FUTURES

Also by Ken Edwards:

POETRY
Good Science: poems 1983–1991 (1992)
eight + six (2003)
Bird Migration in the 21st Century (2006)
No Public Language: Selected Poems 1975-1995 (2006)

PROSE
Nostalgia for Unknown Cities (2007)

Futures

KEN EDWARDS

REALITY STREET

Published by
REALITY STREET
63 All Saints Street, Hastings TN34 3BN
www.realitystreet.co.uk

Cover illustration: *Bacchus and Ariadne* by Titian

Thanks to the Hawthornden Foundation for providing the author
with time and space

Printed & bound in Great Britain
by Lightning Source

2nd printing, 2010

A catalogue record for this book is available from the British
Library

ISBN: 1-874400-13-X (978-1-874400-13-4)

1: She heard the satellite come down

She heard the satellite continue to deviate from its orbit. But how could this be? How could it make sense to say she heard it? Well, it left a trace, which is to say, not really an auditory or visual phenomenon at all but one she could sense as a disturbance pattern "out there". Translated into auditory terms, the trace was a scream, or a banshee wail, with a dying fall to it, somewhere in the stratosphere of attention; visually, it could be described as a long scribble of light searing a path through a galaxy of neurones. But these are just metaphors, description. Essentially, her body plotted the satellite's errant path as it passed overhead unseen, more than a hundred miles above the city. She awoke briefly, then, moisture on her face, bruised. That would have been in the early morning, certainly before it was light.

Strange that she could have dropped off to sleep at all, but she had done so, and it was true that a faint blueness was beginning to stamp out the trapezoidal shape of her attic bedroom window; the shape telling her no less clearly than the intuited trace of the satellite (interfered with by the warble pattern of the pigeons) that she had once again returned from zero — to what, to a waking dream she dreaded? She was still drifting in and out of a zone of terror and unreal beauty, and it was as though her consciousness oscillated in an increasingly frantic rhythm before tipping over into chaos: one moment the world was constricting her, she could touch its four cosy corners (the four corners of her room, in fact) with her bare outstretched fingers; the next she was in a huge starless void between living and dying; and this sequence repeated itself with increasing rapidity.

But soon it would be properly morning. There'd be sunshine, tinged only tinily with foreboding, and that merely the promise of autumn, or its threat. Stupid. Everything would be OK again. In the small grubby kitchen on the first floor, her two golden sisters would be sitting at the table, their body language as she entered suggesting that they'd been talking about her. No reason to suppose they didn't have her best interests at heart. Yet she wanted to escape to the fresh air. And once she had achieved this, what would there be left for her?

•

But that's still in the future. It's the future of this moment. Which is early evening. The evening before the young woman heard the satellite fall.

On the roof warmed by the setting sun, unseasonably, she reclines, bare legs drawn up, her book propped upon them. The sounds are dying down. The school at the end of the lane is silent at this time of day, and even the rumble of traffic, muffled up here, is increasingly interrupted. Now and again, there's a phased drone as an aeroplane passes way overhead, over the city.

The house she and her two companions live in is completely isolated, even though right in the midst of the inner city.

Once, all the housing in the neighbourhood was of this type: three-storeyed, built of dirty yellow brick, no foundations, simply sitting on six foot of rubble above the lost rivers of the city, terraced in row behind row. Mean streets where children played; you see them in sepia photographs preserved in the local history library. The streets remain, in some cases only vestigially; but the children now live in the awesomely beached ocean liners of modern slab and tower block estates that rim the young woman's horizon, their security lights blazing all night, beacons against the grossly imagined unknown.

The jagged edges of the brickwork tell the story of the house's wrenching from its past. Involuntarily detached from its terrace, the last of its sort, it is flanked by nothingness. Or rather, on one side by an impromptu car-park behind chain-link fencing, used by the teachers from the grim faced school.

On the other by a bit of scrubby public garden: a bench whereon frequently an elderly woman might pause to rest her shopping in its wheeled bag; a length of fecally hazardous undergrowth nuzzled by a stray dog or two. On the low brick wall marking the lane's opposite side, someone has laboriously and angrily spelled out in shaky letters of white paint THIS IS NOT A DUMP. Vain protest. Rubbish lines the pavement. The lane itself is narrow, a cul-de-sac off the rat-run, used for parking during the working week, overshadowed by three massive plane trees still weighed down with leaves that autumn is already beginning to strip off.

On the roof, the young woman sees none of this. Below her, the house itself is quiet and empty. Becoming drowsy, she lets the book slip slowly from her fingers.

•

The man gets out of his car, shading his eyes against the low sun as he straightens. Firmly, with a delicate wrist flick, he shuts the door. Slow movement in wind. He's parked in a sort of yard, in a part of the city, south of the river, that frankly makes him uneasy. There's a disused newspaper distribution office, its windows broken. A lorry depot. The graffiti marks are as inscrutable as Arabic texts. Caught on the double strand of barbed wire topping the chain-link fencing, scraps of dirty white polythene stretch and flap, incapable of any further purposive motion. Resistance. Behind him, the line of traffic builds on the rat-run, at the start of the evening rush out of the city, towards the loving suburbs.

The man is young and tall. He is dark-haired, clean-shaven, and wears a lightweight business suit, perhaps too light for the time of year with its nip of future chill threatening to cancel the late sunshine. He knows where he is now. A fallen angel would never look so composed. He has rarely ventured in this part of the city before, but of the anxiety he may feel there is no outward trace.

Perhaps he truly believes himself to be on a mission of noble purpose, rather than one of gratification. It's entirely possible that he is as inscrutable to his own probing as he is to others.

Where has he come from?

Perhaps, again, he works in a high white office, way over on the other side of the river, in the financial district. The buildings there tower in groups, leaving canyons of streets far below, clogged with taxis and motorcycle despatch riders. Tucked into corners are sandwich bars, shops selling fax machines, mobile phones and computers, bookshops stocking only business books and how-to health manuals. Fronting them are marble porticos and brass plates announcing the real presence of the head offices of international merchant banks, or the immense glass-surrounded spaces of contemporary foyers, containing within them actual rain-forests watered by sculptured fountains, the reception desks islanded in the centre of a thick-carpeted clearing. The offices above are reached by jewelled and silent elevators; they are air-conditioned, and filled with computers whose screens are alive with multicoloured figures, decoded by young men and women in laundered shirts and blouses, the men with their ties loosened, speaking rapidly into telephones.

Perhaps. But it's all so different here. Poverty, or, to put it a gentler way, scope for development, speaks out from every direction. Everything seems to him to be broken, or disused, or used for a purpose it was not intended for. Fragments of newspaper move along the pitted ground. Sunlight bounces off corrugated baffles. An elderly woman, making painfully slowly for the pedestrian crossing whose red has already changed to green, skirts suspiciously a loose paving stone.

Somewhere, a white slash in that clear sky describes a far-away jet aircraft hitting the sound barrier.

He turns and walks surely away from his car. He passes (unconcernedly) the chain-link fencing WARNING: GUARD DOG. The designated cur, now emerging from his house of broken brick, runs to the fence, scolds, and scolds again. But the young man merely flickers an impassive look and walks on; soon the dog is left well behind, futilely scolding into the distance.

At the corner is a tobacconist's. He enters. Moments later, he re-emerges with the evening paper, which he funnels and puts to his brow briefly against the sun. He re-orientates himself towards his objective. The house.

Now his anxiety begins to be mingled with sexual excitement. An aura which was born in his groin starts to radiate through every organ and muscle of his body, cancelling their weight. However, there is still no outward sign of his inner angelic rage.

The "unthinkable" creeps into his head then, and becomes thought.

•

The young woman hasn't long returned from work. Her two friends are nowhere to be seen. For the past hour, she's been on her favourite spot, the roof, soaking herself in the slanting light; her book — or rather, her friend Zoo's Tarot book — fallen beside her on the tartan blanket where she lies, drifting into sleep, pulled out of her doze suddenly by the approaching evening. Yesterday she was reading a science-fiction novel, but now she's abandoned this in favour of the Tarot book. Perhaps she wants some clue to Zoo's strange sweet power.

She wears blue shorts, a white singlet; her feet are bare. Starting to get chilly, she thinks to herself, a small tremor blurring the outline of her body. But it isn't just the disappearance of the sun that caused a shiver. She's felt the faint vibration of the doorbell far below, resonating through beam, floorboard, lath and plaster.

Down she climbs the uncertain ladder, through the trapdoor, into her little attic bedroom; then down quickly two flights of uncarpeted stairs in her bare feet, two by two, swinging on the banister at the turn; and, sidling past the bicycle in the narrow hall, opens the front door.

His eyes are the darkest possible. She remembers, and the memory spreads to every part of her body.

"I was just passing," he says, "and I thought I'd call on the offchance. To see how you were." He is serious. His face, which is sharp as a knife if she remembers correctly, is in shadow now. "I needed to apologise."

Her body temporarily weakened, she fails to believe him yet tries to conceal this fact by looking away, examining closely the parked bicycle's handlebars. With her thumb, she pings the bell; the sound is framed within the pause. But after those few moments, she turns her eyes to him again, and says, "Well, come in." Her voice low and uncertain.

Now they're in the kitchen. He has placed his lightweight grey jacket on the back of the chair on which he sits; he's loosened his tie; his white shirt smells of laundering, his thick shining black hair of recent washing. Even the folded newspaper he has been carrying, and now lays on the table in front of him, is fresh.

"I'm sorry — I behaved badly," he reiterates. She does not reply to this; instead, she asks, "Would you like something to drink?" He nods. For him, she gets a can of beer out of the bulky refrigerator.

"So this is where you live," he says, raising the frosted can to his lips. Again, she doesn't reply to his overture, merely sinking to her own chair across the table from him. She doesn't get a drink for herself. Inspecting his perfect cuffs as though he's only just noticed them, he adds: "And you're here, what, squatting? How resourceful! How many of you are there?" His voice is, what do they call it, educated.

Instead of answering, she repeats, catching up on the word of a few minutes ago: "Apologise?"

Too nonchalantly: "Yes, I came to apologise about last week. I hoped — well — I don't know what I hoped. I suppose I haven't any right to hope." Now he smiles briskly, a first attempt that falls just short of his eyes, to indicate that his irony truly masks concern (there are too many levels to him).

"Hope?" she repeats, again, puzzled. "Right?"

There is a silence for a bit, while she contemplates the meaning of this sudden affectation of speech he has adopted. Were she more alert to the possibility, she could have latched onto the fact of his nervousness. But the imbalance of power in the relationship prevents this insight.

For no other reason than to break the awkward silence, she picks up the dessert spoon that happens to be resting on the table and, leaning over with a rush of boldness, holds it close to his face. "Speak into the microphone please. Tell me, when did you first realise you were an utter, an utter, an utter. . . ?" But, boldness dissolving into repetition, she blushes slightly, at her own daring and sublimated desire. Yes, it is desire. And it's betrayed her. Like the face of an angel, is the phrase that builds itself inexplicably in her mind. Knowledge is in that face. Oddly, she now wants to laugh. But doesn't. She is in danger of betraying herself. In fact, she already has. The gesture she intended as defiance has come out as collusion. That's why it collapsed, really. Her laughter, then, would be partly at least a laughter of irritation with herself.

As for him, he looks as if he doesn't know whether to laugh or cry, though of course neither is a serious proposition. He's ice not fire. Maybe he can't help it. So, selecting mild annoyance as the appropriate response, he says OK I admit I was wrong.

She actually feels sorry for him now. When the hint of a smile begins to steal, unwanted, across her face, he takes this as a signal, and laughs shortly. And so does she.

He says: "OK, are we friends? Listen, I'm really interested, I wasn't just asking the question out of awful politeness. Are you squatting here?"

Putting the embarrassing spoon down, she explains:

"Well, I dunno, I think of it as just living. This house was dying. Nobody had lived in it for some years. I think it was going to be pulled down. The council had pulled down all the other houses in the street. By the time they came to this one — well, fashions changed. They were being criticised for destroying the area and building tower blocks. But they didn't know what to do. There was no money left. They just abandoned this one. We occupied it, that's all. Took a month to paint and decorate, renewing plasterwork a bit. A patch job. We'd have been homeless. Me and Dee, and the others, who've now left."

I admire your application, he says. Though it sounds impossibly phony, she chooses to ignore this, and continues:

"There's just three of us now. Zoo, who's a student, she's here temporarily. And Dee. And myself. Zoo and Dee won't be back till later, I suppose. Just us and the mice."

She even begins to explain, she doesn't know why, just chattering through nervousness she supposes, how she secured the top floor bedroom with the low sloping ceiling, a nest secluded from and yet overlooking the metropolitan sprawl. And now the air in the kitchen starts to lose its charged quality. She describes how the trapdoor to the roof happens to be in the ceiling of her tiny bedroom, making of the roof an annexe to her personal domain.

Immediately, he begs to see it. He is like a little boy, yet hot power shoots from his eyes to her eyes to make her dizzy, so that she can't really look straight at him for too long. Yes, if you want, she finds herself saying.

•

Her memory calls up a damp, summery night, perhaps a week ago. A garden, in the suburbs of the city, south of its great sprawl. That was the first, and only other time they had met. They were talking in somebody's abandoned "summer-house" — actually a half demolished brick shed among the sycamores of that long garden. She had had too much to drink; the party was a soft susurrus behind them, in the house. How had she found herself at this party? It was too long a story. She knew hardly anybody, and he had offered himself as guardian.

He had placed his strong hand on her cheek, just lightly. He said: "When I was a child, I'd be lying in bed ... alone ... it's all dark ... and I'd think, what if I just stopped breathing, just like that?"

And she remembered now (memory nesting within memory) how it was then, and quickly began to choke; the air was thick, like glue or something; there was nobody else around. She panicked; her small hands, resting on a wooden rail, felt moist; in front of her, a blackbird hopped into evening shadows from which emanated powerfully the scent of rotten wood. He cupped her cheeks between his hands, big ones but slender, and looked into her eyes with his dark ones, wonderingly, and with increasing desire; she was sobbing for breath.

•

But now they are both on the roof, in the cool clear air.

The roof of this house, where she spends so many secret hours, is the inverse of a ridge, in other words a trough: the double bank of grey slates, retaining heat still from the day's sunshine, rising to truncated half gables on either side, a narrow valley floor between, and parapets protecting this enclave front and back. So they're completely shut off from everything except the deepening sky above, and the pigeons that strut and flutter, making their home beneath some broken slates which are whitened with their droppings. It's been a better than usual summer, and this sun-trap is where she's spent much of it. And the freakishly warm autumn, Indian summer the papers call it, that now ensues. Perhaps Dee and Zoo have ventured up here on occasion, drinking beer and laughing while they peel off and toast their calves. But mostly she's come here alone with a book, climbing through the square wood-framed opening that interrupts the slated slope.

It's quiet and peaceful, and best of all it's hers. Her private domain, her paradise garden in the sky, secluded from the city's faraway intercourse. When she took two weeks off from work this was where she spent most of her time, reading, devouring book after book. The sounds were strangely far away, including the noises of unseen children in the school at the end of the lane. Sometimes she heard them screaming in the playground, their howls echoing from wall to wall; at other times, she heard their rhythmic, eerie chanting, the numbers inexorably rising: One, two, three ... nineteen, twenty, twenty-one ... ninety-eight, ninety-nine, a hundred.... So far away.

And now here they are, she and the strange man; side by

side, they lie on the blanket spread on the slates. Why has she agreed to bring him up here, to violate her space? She had to let him come through her bedroom, and that felt uncomfortable; she couldn't look at his eyes. Up the rickety ladder, she first, his hot presence right below. It also excites her to make herself vulnerable, she supposes — an ignoble emotion.

He says: "And do your friends, what's their names, Dee and Zoo, do they come up here too?" Yes, sometimes, she says. "I bet this is good for sunbathing," he says. It's been a wonderful summer, she replies. "Do you ever, eh, I bet you sunbathe nude sometimes," he says, grinning charmingly. "I mean, it's amazing, nobody can see you here. Except from an aircraft, I suppose." She's embarrassed; she laughs. He repeats: "Nude, the three of you, it's OK, you don't have to tell me."

Now they can see only the sky above them; the parapets hide the city. To the west, a hint of high cirrus begins to be flecked and striated with rose; the parapet shadow creeps over them. To deflect the conversation from an unwanted area, she starts to talk about herself, to place herself as it were. Leaning on one elbow, in front of the setting sun, her face shadowing his, she draws an imaginary orbit on one of the slates, circling its square. "This is where I am, being pulled in," she explains; she means pulled in by the possibility of total engagement, human relationships, jobs, responsibilities. "But really I'd like to be out there": that is, pointing up the slant of the roof to the sky. Suddenly, there is so much space. With a shock, the infant has learned local habitation. And then to inhabit a margin, to learn to negotiate that. She floats; what's this about, is it about eyeballing her greatest fears, is it about coming of age, is it about freedom? She pushes herself to confront it, that terror/beauty, lying face up on the roof before the sky and feeling, not for the first time, as though she were clinging upside down to the surface of the planet, pressed to it by nothing more substantial than a trust in gravity, the fathomless sky below her. She is afraid, again, of the space in which she finds herself; her body can't touch its boundaries, and anxiety wells unbidden out of that space. How often has she lain there, centripetally pinned, terrified/exhilarated by the blue void beneath her? And then it subsides, and she is back in her familiar rooftop lair with the soothing pigeons.

Another memory: in the city, an elderly woman, terrified, at the edge of the forecourt of a petrol station, unable to cross. She responds to her fear. Just accompany her across all that space. Her body, without boundaries, reaches out to another. She becomes the stranger then. Who unwittingly brings comfort, precisely because of her otherness.

So now, as she talks, she feels that the warmth they lie on is a field of force that binds them together, and this odd feeling creates a silence for some minutes. "I understand," he tells her, and it thrills her to imagine that this might possibly be true. Then he raises an arm to point, what is it, the steady brightness of Venus ("the evening star" he says); it's almost as though he made it by pointing, because she hasn't noticed it rise and flare till he did that; he wonders aloud whether they will see the satellite moving across the sky.

What satellite?

It's in the paper that he's left on the kitchen table below. He relates the back-page story from memory: a brief update on the progress of a landmapping satellite that is falling out of orbit; it was a polar orbit, more than a hundred miles above the earth, enabling the satellite to track every square mile of the earth as it turned, monitoring land and ocean with remote sensing cameras, both optical and infra-red, why, they'd be able to pick up this very roof, but what happened, something went wrong, an instrument failed, the satellite started to deviate from its orbit ... but she's not listening to his words now, only to the way that they place themselves in the air between them. Her heart's beating quickly; she bursts into a brilliant silence almost of revelation. They are no longer two beings isolated from each other, her racing thought tells her, there's a presence they generate which is their proper being.

He's got onto a different subject. He's moving his hands as he speaks, big hands but slender, with long, strong fingers, like a violinist's. What's he talking about now, his work? She knows now that he works in the financial district on the other side of the river that bisects the city, in a big building filled with computer screens whose variegated light he watches for signs of changes in fortunes. Commodities? Minerals and fruits of the earth?

Nothing so simple. A premonition of a smile is on his lips again. His white shirt is almost blue in the fading light. No. Futures.

"What futures?" she demands, puzzled.

"Not," he says, picking up the Tarot book abandoned on the slates, "this stuff."

No, he is talking about true absences. The prices of things rather than the things themselves. That is (he corrects himself, tossing the paperback onto the slates again, where it slides to the centre trough), even further removed than that. The absence of an absence, you might say. The ghost of a ghost. What he does, he explains, is to predict what the hypothetical price of a hypothetical consignment of a certain commodity will be — in so many months' time — and advise his clients where to put their money. On which he takes a percentage.

So what happens when the corn or the cotton, or whatever it is, is finally delivered? Oh, it never comes to that. (That ghostly smile again.) "We don't actually get bales of cotton delivered by the lorryload to our office. We've sold our right to buy them, hopefully at a profit, before then. It's a risk, it's like gambling."

She: And do you always win?

She's got her eyes closed, lying on the blanket, but what she can imagine only frightens her, and makes her body start to tremble. (Is it the notion of absence that bothers her? Or is she merely feeling the chill? Maybe she should just go downstairs and put on her sweater and jeans. It may be a freak autumn, but it's still autumn, and evening is drawing in.) Afraid he'll notice the tremor in her legs, she opens her eyes to accept his image. But he's no longer lying at her side. He's standing at the far end, his back to her, leaning over the parapet. He turns to her, and he's even grinning now. First, her eyes can see only him, and then they can't see him at all. As though the dark light of evening itself is now a veil.

The conversation is becoming unreal. Maybe she has fallen asleep, and is dreaming it.

He: Yes. I always win. Or I have always won up to now. Well, often enough as makes no difference. It's cyclic, the shift in prices, you learn to predict it, you get a feel for the cycles.

She lifts herself off the blanket and goes to join him. How lovely those city lights from afar, now she can see them, and the overhead traffic of white and winking green and red lights — the flight path into the big international airport beyond the city.

They watch for a while.

He: You don't sound very enthusiastic about my work.

She: I'm sure it's very interesting, and exciting and all that.

(Pause.)

He: So what is it, do you think what I'm doing is immoral?

She: I don't know why you're bringing in that stuff.

He: What, you mean morality?

She: Morality ... that's what people like you have invented to ... make sense of ... what you do. Don't talk to me about morality.

People like you. Why did she say that, why the sudden need to distance herself?

He: That's an odd notion.

She: All I'm saying's I never brought up morality in the first place, you did.

(Silence.)

He: So what shall we talk about?

She: I like the buildings, there.

What she is pointing at is the horizon — which has always invaded her metabolism with its promise, a promise whose fulfilment is eternally, deliciously postponable. On the left of this darkening skyline are two tall office blocks. Then the housing estate, warm glows already at many of its windows, the lights in the centre stairwells coming on one by one. In the middle, the distant communications tower with its red warning light perched atop its antennae, eternally blinking at the aircraft. On the right, more office blocks and the already floodlit dome of the seventeenth century cathedral.

He: What do you like about them?

She (after thought): I find them comforting. That they're always there. Don't you agree?

He: Well ... I don't know what you mean. What goes up must come down.

She: That's true, of course.

He: Look over there. I think you can just about see the building where I work. The cathedral's in the way.

As he speaks he touches her suddenly. But she flinches.

He is annoyed at her instinctive reaction. The word "precious" comes to his mind, in all its shades of meaning.

After a while, she says, "I'm sorry. But you just can't assume ..." Defeated, she begins again; it costs her a great deal of effort. "People like you ..." (that distancing again) "... I expect, don't get me wrong, think you can buy your way everywhere with charm."

Oh, he says sarcastically, so what's your price, then?

It's stupid and uncalled for, but her anger only manages to push against the surfaces of her body, causing it to tremble the more. What she really wants to say is, OK, does he want to speculate on it, is that what will get him off? But even the potential of the language is too heavy to leave her throat.

So she tries to calm down, remembering the last time, in that garden, how she couldn't breathe. How he'd said, what if it was impossible to breathe, and just his saying it made her start to choke. And how it was just at that moment that he came to her, when she was defenceless and too drunk to think straight anyway. But there's no excuse now. She breathes slowly and deliberately deeply, therefore. "Let's just enjoy the evening. It's so beautiful up here. You could change the world just by wishing, at least that's what it feels like."

He: So you want to change the world?

She: I think so.

He: Because you're so moral, aren't you? (stressing and

elongating the "so" to the point of absurdity) despite your dis-
avowal?

(Silence.)

He (incredulously): You think there's any hope of that? Just
by wishing?

She: You're the one who brought up hope in the first place.
Morality and hope.

Now she's discovered something about him, something she
didn't know before, and possibly he doesn't know yet: that he
suffers from the illusion that he is in control of events. He
thinks every possibility can be modelled, and that the model is
equivalent to reality. This is his strength, which is obviously
attractive to her, but also his ultimate weakness: that he, the
apparent realist, is engaged in making structures out of unreal-
ity. And also he feeds off his environment, there's nothing at
the centre and source of his being. When he gives her his
energy, which awes and attracts her, it isn't really giving at all
but inadvertent reflection; he's an accumulator and that fact
will destroy him.

As for him, he sees only her body now, the limbs unencum-
bered, from which the afternoon's sunshine is just slowly withdrawing. Her soft thighs soft golden down. He tries to put it
out of his mind, but can't.

"Actually, my dearest darling," she is saying, thoughtfully
but not without an unaccustomed irony, "I like the world a
whole lot better than you do. Even if I want to change it and
you don't."

He: Why?

She: Because … something is always happening for the first
and last time.

He: Why did you say that?

She: I don't know. (She actually doesn't, or can't articulate
it.)

He: What does it mean?

She: It means freedom.

He (sarcastically): Well, we'll all drink to that. Freedom, I'll
buy that. I tell you what freedom is: it's that we're all by nature

Nothing. You know what I'm saying? We start with zero. And then along come teachers and politicians and churches and whatnot, trying to drill us into being like everybody else if we're stupid enough. The thing is not to be that stupid. Or ... I expect you think it's something wonderful and wild and romantic? You don't realise you're already free, you're too afraid.

She (angrily): Yeah, free like you, to screw whoever you want for whatever you can get?

He: So now we have it. You *are* into the morality of it. That's not fair. I'm capable of giving too. I'll give you anything you like.

She: Beg your pardon?

He: Look, you don't really want to live in a dump like this, let's be frank. I could find you a place to live, somewhere really nice.

She (incredulously): You could?

He: Yeah. Christ, I can afford it, I make millions. More than I can spend, I'm not really into spending.

She: Oh, you're a what's it, an altruist. A benefactor, a philanthropist.

(Silence.)

She: No, of course you're not. I really find this quite incredible.

He: Sorry?

She: Sorry, OK then, you said you were sorry, I forgot. You want to make amends? Forget about setting me up in a nice little flat, if that's what you're on about, too much trouble, really. Why don't you just give me your money. The money you get from the future.

He: You should've asked me nicely.

Though a smile is fixed to his lips, his voice is thick and caked for the first time this evening with an emotion ugly enough to be just something abstract. But that's something she noticed the time before, in the garden, even through her haze of drunkenness, that he has two voices, a sweet neutral thin one that he uses for exposition, and this clotted one that kind of sits behind it; and the danger point for anyone has arrived precisely when he slips from one into the other. At some other time, that would be interesting, she thinks. But now she has to extricate herself from this, yet something drives her on, uncharacteristically.

She: You think you impressed me the other week, in the garden, at the party? It's laughable. Why did you really come here? Give me your money if you really want to impress me. What've you got on you?

He: You're barmy.

She: Give me your shit-energy, or something.

He: I'll give it to you. I'll give it to you all right.

And now it's too late to draw back. Just like in the damp suburban garden, a blackbird hopping away unconcerned. Or worse, despising her. She feels as though she has always been despised. Even up here now, on her very own peaceful roof.

All at once he slaps her across the face. It's not a hard slap, but the sting of it so shocks her she doesn't even burst into tears for a few moments.

She: You bastard.

The spectacle of her weakness excites him. He wants to possess that weakness, maybe because he imagines he suffers from an excess of strength. Or, deeper down, he wants her weak strength to fill his secret weakness.

He pulls her down onto the slates. He has understood nothing. She hears herself pleading, please, take care, no, no don't, don't be stupid. Contradictory messages. The fact is, she's suddenly realised, too late, despite his superficial cleverness, his assurance, his occasional wit, he is stupid. Too late. The final desolation: that the protective magic of her roof seclusion has failed. Utterly quiet now, he has her close, his warm breath smelling of the earlier beer, boiling up from his gut. He hits her again. I just want to tell you something, he is saying, in his clotted voice, almost pathetically, all his composure suddenly gone, you just don't listen to what I'm saying. And in the evening air, from one of the other houses, the scent of frying bacon. Far away, a dog barks, and barks again, unconsoled.

He grabs at her singlet, pulling it down over one shoulder

to expose the bare dull shine of it; now he thrusts a solid thigh between her bare legs. For Christ's sake, she sobs. She's crying because the vision has vanished, and it's her fault. But she doesn't really make much sound. You don't listen, do you, he's saying. There is a sudden clattering; it's three pigeons moving rapidly away from the top of the roof into the sky. He forces down her shorts; she kicks, perhaps hurts him. He's swearing under his breath, because he's not really hard enough yet, he has to tear his way through, and that even hurts him too. But in the space of an instant he has become completely alien and strong. His slender fingers gripping her throat.

It happens for about ten minutes, she thinks later. Or was it just ten seconds? One, two, three … five hundred and ninety-eight, five hundred and ninety-nine, six hundred, she hears, clear as a bell, the ghost voices of the children chanting in the empty school. The rape. That's what it is, isn't it? That's what a bewigged, berobed judge in a solemn court of law in the solemnest centre of this city would call it. Or rather, the alleged rape. And then there'd be the defence lawyer, who's really on the attack: "Do you seriously expect people to believe you when you say you meant nothing by inviting my client up to your roof?… Now you say the previous week the same thing happened?… With my client?… At a party?… And you don't remember where?… Your memory isn't exactly infallible, is it?… And you did what about it?… Oh, nothing.… Of course, you'd had a great deal to drink then? … And even though, so you say, the same thing happened a week before, you still invited my client?… Now tell the court what you were wearing.… I see, so even though it was an autumn evening and getting chilly.…"

Rape. But it doesn't feel real now, because there's nobody around to define it. And already, already she is beginning to forget it, even at that moment, mercifully, the memory is starting to blur.…

She lies weeping, shorts and pants dragged to her calves, singlet ripped, in the roof valley — is there blood? And he leans against the parapet once more, buttoning his fly, chest heaving, head bowed, darkness shadowing his face, tie askew, white shirt gleaming crumpled in the dying light. His voice is thickened still:

"It's what you wanted, after all, isn't it?"

(Silence. Slowly, painfully she pulls up her clothing.)

The moon is in the sky.

And then she goes for him. The action is totally unpredictable; even she didn't predict it. Afterwards, she couldn't fathom where the energy had exploded from. But it did. Blind rage. He's taken completely by surprise as, muscles taut, she cannons towards him. So he slips. The expression on his face is almost comical.

He cracks his head on the side of the parapet, an almighty crack what a crack indeed, moments later she's wanting to be sick just from the thought of the sound, and he goes down without another, sliding into the roof's valley, sliding effortlessly like dancers do. For a moment he's completely still, then the tremor starts. A hideous, blind spasm that vibrates his body rhythmically. She watches, fascinated, his foot: it twitches every so often. The periods between twitches are getting longer now. She notices dispassionately what expensive shoes he wears, classy black brogues, quite new really, made to measure probably. And slowly dark liquid starts pulsing from the side of his head. She is squatting on the slates, head in hands, a small chuckle coming from nowhere to vibrate her own body, muttering over and over: It's the end of a beautiful summer.

That seems funny to her.

•

Something is always happening for the first and last time. Why did she say that? What did she mean? A sunset; the evening star; the chance meeting (what chance?) of two people on a rooftop, in a decaying part of a great city. Bacon frying and dogs barking beneath the moon. A yellowing leaf at the top of one of three plane trees in the lane trembles suddenly in the breeze, detaches itself and begins its non-linear descent to the street. Beyond the stratosphere, a satellite that has crossed the earth's equator a hundred times unaccountably slips out of its orbit.

•

In a different rhythm now, her lungs dilate. Where are Dee and Zoo? Surely they must be back by now? Her loneliness is intolerable.

He doesn't move at all. The police. Call the police, that's what you do. But she can't bear it. If Dee was here she'd get her to do that, Dee's good at taking charge in an emergency. She begins painfully to crawl over to his slumped body. Is he breathing? She doesn't know. She puts her hand on his chest, but has to withdraw it. His mouth is slightly parted, but her mouth won't go there. Not in a million years. She recoils, unwilling even to look at him now.

It's all over. He remains sprawled by the parapet in a terrifyingly unnatural posture, his face suddenly grey, his hair matted. A dark stain has begun to spread over the slates.

One slate has been dislodged by his flailing foot. It has slid into the gutter between the roofs, where it rests. She picks it up and looks at it in her hand, as though she has lost the sense of what it is. Before long, however, she is replacing it carefully into the slot it has vacated, wedging it in with the other slates. Her exaggerated care over this meaningless manoeuvre is a way of displacing fear; specifically, the fear that she will be drawn unwillingly to look into those eyes that she knows still stare into vacancy — as one who stands on a high ledge and knows that a single look down may prove fatal. Or perhaps who clings to a rooftop, eyes glazed against the void above.

And now into the silence begins to settle a whirring noise. Dusk has come. Above her head, a machine appears. A police helicopter, white and red lights twinkling deeply, crosses the newly risen moon.

How could they know, so quickly? Standing up, she waves at the aircraft with both arms. But its appearance is mere coincidence. The men inside her haven't seen what has taken place on the rooftop far below them. They are probably on their way back to base after surveying the evening rush hour traffic. In a few moments the helicopter is gone again.

Stiffly, looking impassively ahead of her, she reaches for the tartan blanket; she spreads it over the body, taking care to cover it completely.

She's downstairs in the kitchen. It's beginning to get too dark to see without switching on the light. She does so. The jacket. It's still hanging on the back of the chair.

She searches the breast pocket, the inside pockets; pulls out a wallet and a chequebook. The cheques are personalised: Mr John and Mrs Sonia Newman. She reads the twin names with neither emotion nor recognition. The wallet contains credit cards, a driving licence, all in the name of John Newman, and a small crumpled colour photograph of a woman about her own age, standing on a bridge, smiling. This woman is dark, pretty.

She's telling herself to keep calm at all costs. In the bathroom, she changes out of her torn and bloodied clothes, and douses warm water over herself (the plumbing sighs and clanks, as it always does, deep within the bowels of the old house). The mirror.

She sees a small oval face, its delicacy swollen by tears, the dark eyes that once were lustrous now dulled, the short dark hair tousled. Her face, is it really hers? It's as if she's looking at it for the first time. As if it's the face of a total stranger. With difficulty, she tears herself away from its wonder. She goes to the toilet. It hurts. She puts on her short bath robe.

Now what? She steels herself to climb the ladder for the last time, and without looking at the hideous shape under the tartan blanket to fling the jacket up onto the roof. Then, closing the trapdoor carefully above her, she climbs back down into her bedroom. She puts the ladder away into the landing cupboard where it always goes. By now, her sobs have died away, but she still takes the time to sit on her bed, close her eyes, and continue deliberately to breathe deeply and slowly, once twice three times.

Still in her bath robe, she gets under her bedcovers and lies there with the light out staring at the shape of her window. Sometimes the window seems to fill her entire consciousness, its presence taunting her with all the thickness and materiality of the objects of the world; and at other times it's as if it were a mile away and she drifting even further from it, even further from the faint orange tinge of the street's sodium light, out of direct sight somewhere below, pregnant with evanescence, her only connection with the world of appearances. Her mind oscillates between the two states.

•

The satellite moved over the waters of the earth. It was as though she saw through its very imaging systems. She saw open pits and dumps of waste material. She saw the field pattern of distant agricultures. She discovered the deep rock strata, fossil water; heat-emitting strips of settlement, with their bright lights of casinos and hotels, winding their way through foreign basalt deserts; dark areas whose immense sweep no single individual could have grasped. She discerned the city in which she lived, slipping into darkness, brilliant points of light winking on. The quality of the information was too much for her. She felt as though she were a string of numbers on a computer disk. She was porphyry copper; she was right at the beginning of the information flow of a long night.

•

She didn't hear the voices of Dee and Zoo when they returned, the worse for drink, much later. But outside her window, had she stayed awake, she might have been startled every few minutes by a small golden shape that appeared in the darkness, twisted and banked, catching the sodium glow in its fall and rapid evanescence. One by one, the leaves from the top of the plane tree nearest to the house were beginning to float to the street below, each one describing its unique path.

•

The satellite was a hot bird that scintillated. It moved slowly over the water and the city. Inside the satellite, it was dark. Dark and clean and pristine. There were endless corridors. She paced through them. The darkness was also quiet. But her mind was clear. She called the corridors "galleries". One after another, they slipped by, each identical to the one before; she could just make out the gentle curve to the left ahead, always the perfectly round doorway.

No, it wasn't completely quiet. Wasn't that a faint pattering she could hear? But when she stopped to listen, the sound stopped also. She started walking again, and again she heard the tiny sound. It seemed to come from behind her. She stopped, it stopped. She turned around, not afraid. Slowly she began to retrace her steps. This time there was no sound. She stepped through the circular doorway she had recently come through. A small black shape, two dim points of light, reflected from whatever ambient dimness there was around. It was a dog, she realised. It stood stock still, watching her. She knew it would retreat if she went any further towards it. She was not frightened. It was as if dumb love emanated from the dog, even though it did look scary. Once again she turned and stepped back through the doorway, continuing in her original direction. She heard the dog begin to follow.

Now the interior of the satellite began to be haunted by an increasing number of sights and sounds.

A brilliant window opened in the corridor wall on her right. About four feet square. She saw a garden. Its light splashed her face in the dimness of the corridor. The light of the green grass, left unmowed, mingled with pale oxlips, primroses and daisies, as though it were perpetual spring. Grass and weeds invaded a crooked path that led to a crumbling wooden bird-house on a pole. Rhododendron bushes. And beyond, standard roses beginning to bud crimsonly against a dark hedge. Then, beyond the hedge...

She touched the glass; it was cold to her stroking fingertips.

She could almost smell the garden. She knew it, she had been there before. She could hear the low hum of its insects, and the complicated songs of its birds. It was out there somewhere.

Slowly, she stumbled on through the passage or gallery, seeking the entrance to the garden. Behind her she could hear the dog trot. But the entrance could not be found.

Instead, she came to another window set in the wall. She saw its light and heard its murmur before she came to it. Through this window, which was identical to the first, the colours danced in regimented patterns on banks of computer screens. The colours were figures representing money, or the promise/threat of money, updating themselves from moment to moment. Monotonously, a man's echoing voice could be heard reciting an endless stream of meaningless (to her) numbers. She smelt ozone, an electric smell. The banks of screens were in rows behind one another, slightly at a diagonal to her point of view, but nobody was attending them. However, in the background, at the end of one of the rows, she could make out a young woman, pretty, with dark hair, dressed in a white blouse and black skirt, writing with a red felt tip marker on a white board. Although the board had already filled up with her figures, she continued to write very rapidly over what she had already written, thus compounding the jumble. It would not be long before the white board became a mass of red, scantily streaked with white. And what then?

Ghost murmurs surrounded her in the darkness, and from afar, the constant purr of telephones ringing. The ghost voices whispered danger. But the dog, still a steady ten yards behind, would protect her.

Onwards she went. Now she realised that the reason the corridor constantly curved to the left was that it — and she — was spiralling inward, to the "heart" of the satellite. For the curve was getting tighter. "I'm getting close to the explanation," she thought to herself, but the thought terrified her.

The voices and the telephones, to which were now added frantic footsteps as of people rushing from one side to the other, began to become unbearable. But presently she was at the end of the corridor: a door ahead of her, a steel door. What frightful thing was on the other side of that door? She reached to touch it.

•

Eye, she said, I'm Eye. She peered at her face in the bathroom mirror. She could hear the cheerful sounds of Dee and Zoo getting breakfast ready in the kitchen. Sunlight on the mirror. Mussed dark hair, oval face, hers. Not a stranger's, no. Why did she have to reassure herself of this by repeating her name? She'd looked at that face in the mirror recently, when?

She'd woken, in her bed, in her bath robe. Nameless fear, its object unknown. That's why she repeated her name, the first that came to her. The name of a stranger. Don't talk to strangers.

I am Eye, she said, whispering it now, and I live in this house. With Dee and Zoo. They're my friends. So nothing's wrong. (But she still didn't convince herself.) There's something terrible she has to tell them. What? No. It was just a dream. A bad dream. Spiralling into it. And in the early hours a shriek, no, not a shriek, not even a sound.

Bruises on her thighs though, why?

Can't remember. What can't she remember? That's what she can't remember.

The sun was shining.

•

Yesterday's newspaper was still on the kitchen table when Eye came down for breakfast. She looked at it briefly, wondering vaguely how it had got there. She was certain she had not bought it — indeed, it was not a newspaper she ever bought — and neither Zoo nor Dee ever bought a paper of any sort. She remembered that she'd had peculiar dreams; images of them struggled, but failed, to form themselves into a real being. She reminded herself that days earlier she had resolved to buy a notebook in which she would write her dreams. All at once the house, damp to its non-existent foundations, was filled with the echoes language had left behind.

Something's happened, she told herself, then realised what an odd thought this was, decoupled from the rest of her being, as it were. A lost memory, struggling in vain to re-form.

So she sat at the table, picked up and pretended to start reading the paper, as a way of giving her psyche time to reintegrate itself.

When she'd woken, she had forgotten where she was. A common enough feeling, this disorientation on waking, but normally it didn't last more than a moment or two. Now she could rationalise again: she was Eye, and she had to go to work this morning, and these two were Zoo and Dee, with whom she shared an almost derelict house. Yet the rationalisations did not make complete sense. The strangeness did not resolve itself as it usually did. Another reason she pretended to read the paper, therefore, was as a way of avoiding conversation with Zoo and Dee, in case she inadvertently gave away her sense of disorientation, and alarmed them unduly.

Dee, however, was grumbling, "... cheese on toast, the cheese was that thick it all messed up the grill ..." when suddenly, unable to ignore Eye's silence at the table, she broke off: "How are you feeling?" she enquired, her tone not altogether sympathetic. Eye paused, thinking for a moment, laying down the uncomprehended paper. This demanded care. She smiled. "Like a ghost."

Dee nodded briskly: "You look like a ghost."

Zoo said: "What is a ghost? It is a name, I think. Ghosts are, you know, the names we bear, ja? I think so. Fifty years ago, there was no entities, I mean no consciousness bearing our own names. Fifty years from now," (she shrugged, using her coffee mug as an extension of her personality), "again there will be no such persons. Only the names, like dry leaves blowing in the lane out there. Ghosts."

Zoo, the German student, had come to stay at the beginning of their idyllic summer. She had transformed the household, not perhaps in obvious ways, but slowly and subtly. With her heavy eyeshadow, patchouli fragrance, leather, and silver bracelets she had seemed like a witch; with her rich, terrific laughter she had filled the house with delight and mystery. (Or: "Funny, she is," was Dee's succinct verdict.) An image came to Eye (concentrating on holding her newspaper steady) of her and Dee returning home on a still summer night, Dee bearing a six-pack and demanding video, Zoo speaking poetry by Goethe. It was a welcome return.

Now Dee was laughing her own raucous laugh, almost falling off her perch (one of the three ill-assorted and rickety wooden kitchen chairs) with the shaking. She imitated the way Zoo spoke ("It iss a name, I sink") before hugging the girl's shoulders with one careless arm to make sure that the peaks of uncertainty generated by this parody were dampened, to make it clear that absolutely no harm was intended, that she was just *being Dee.* (Zoo, pacified, grinned.) "Speak for yourself, dear," continued Dee, "but in fifty years' time I plan to be an eccentric eighty-year old spinster with twelve cats. OK?" Secretly, she thought Zoo's German accent was completely wonderful.

Suddenly she got up, returned to the grill where toast was smoking. Cursing softly to herself, she fanned away unceremoniously the clouds that were beginning to disperse into the air of the kitchen. She rushed with the grill-pan to the sink, already piled with crockery, and commenced fiercely to scrape with a knife at the blackened slices, sending sooty powder over the crocks to coat them with a delicate fur. "Why do we live in such squalor?" she almost shouted, her anger, so quickly returning after giving way briefly to generosity, yet with a measure of half-acknowledged self-parody. Then, returning to the table wildly with the knife, "And you know what, this house stinks. This house stinks of man's piss!" (banging the knife down on the table in unison with her last word, for emphasis).

Eye began to be alarmed. What was she talking about? Dee, sensing this, added quietly, "Oh, I am sorry. I didn't mean ... anything."

But cradling her mug gently with both hands, between

reflective sips, Zoo unconcernedly said, "Ghosts. There may be four of us in this house, you know."

At that, Eye's heart started to jump profusely. She started quietly to cry, and to tremble. She didn't know why.

Dee, misunderstanding at once, as she always did, immediately came round the table to put her arm around her: "Oh heavens, I'm sorry, I'm truly sorry." In reality, despite her abrasiveness, this small untidy woman would do nothing consciously to hurt either Eye or Zoo, rather would she mutilate herself. On the other hand, that in itself was perhaps the most frightening thing about her. They for their part didn't know quite what to do about her, she was so often a cat hoping for some pigeons to be set among. They'd be drinking quietly in the hideous pub with the overloud jukebox at the far end of the lane, all three huddled together for solidarity in the corner half hidden by the white pillars, when little by little Dee's voice would begin to shoot up a few decibels going on about this that or the other — it never seemed to matter what the issue was, the price and availability of artichokes in the Sunday market a few blocks away, or the government's taxation policy, her dark voice comprehended and enveloped it all — until she was definitely in what Zoo termed her "reckless phrase". Then they knew the "phrase" would last all evening, it was no use trying to put a stop to it. She'd go up to this fellow at the bar, perhaps picking him at random. No, not at random, he'd be the good-looking one, and sitting down next to him on an empty bar stool, clicking her coins on the counter, she'd turn round and say, "Hi, I'm Dee. That's easy to remember, isn't it?" What kind of line is that, wondered Eye. And so that would be it, she'd be talking to him all evening, frightening him probably, until Zoo and Eye finish their drinks, fend off the last bantering comments from his friends (wishing they had her extraordinary self assurance), return to the house. Eye waits while Zoo fumbles outside with the key, lit by the solitary sodium street lamp. The wealth of the street's detail fades as it fans out beyond this amber zone; finally Zoo lets them both into the damp smelling hall, they edge their way past the parked bike. A car reverses, its tail lights rubies. An aeroplane is freeze framed on the video, white static ripping it in half.

They would know better than to expect Dee back that evening, then. The rule of the house was, no men. That is, no men in the house. Actually, it was Dee's rule, she'd made it up, the others had just gone along with it. The consequence of it was that Dee frequently stayed out, and Zoo and Eye had the place to themselves.

Eye continued crying, perplexing both herself and Dee, who glumly returned to the fragmented and cooling toast, sharing it out with Zoo. There was silence for a bit, broken only by the quiet sobs and two unsynchronised lots of chewing. For Eye, the moment was passing, the moment of confidence. Soon, she would never be able to grasp it again. In front of her still, the newspaper, slightly smudged now, spread, not fresh, emanating dull heat and the faint smell of ink.

Zoo remarked between munches that she (Eye) did not normally buy this paper. But Eye's attention had been caught, and she didn't respond for a moment. Her dream returned to her, as she read:

SPACE THREAT

A runaway satellite is expected to re-enter the earth's atmosphere today or tomorrow and pieces of it may crash at undetermined locations, military tracking officials said in Colorado Springs.

"That's it. I dreamed about this," she muttered, pensively. She cleared her throat, and the others smiled encouragingly.

"I woke up with this sense of fear, or foreboding," she explained. "It must've been this, I had a nightmare about it. But actually, it was more than a nightmare."

Dee suggested kindly that she had not really been herself this past week. Perhaps it was not wise to go to work this morning. She mentioned a mystery illness that had been much talked about in a magazine she'd recently read, which Eye ought to beware of. But Eye was not listening, because she was trying to recall her dream, because she wanted to tell her two friends about it.

Something had happened. She'd been really tired last night. Tired from work, that was it. She had been reading on the roof, catching the last of the sunshine. Perhaps she was reading this paper? She'd fallen asleep on the roof. Then what happened? The next thing, she was in the bathroom looking at her reflection in the mirror, feeling utterly miserable.

That was just it, interposed Dee excitedly, sudden inexplicable feelings of unhappiness, the magazine article had told you all about it. She shouldn't worry too much, but she shouldn't go to work either.

Eye: And I went to bed and dreamed I was in the satellite, or I *was* the satellite, just falling, falling out of orbit. And I could hear it. I woke up in the wee small hours and I could sort of hear a scream, something like a scream and something like a flash of lightning, the satellite falling down.

Zoo: So what you reckon ziss dream means?

Eye thought for a moment. She said: "If it was a dream. There was also something about the future. That's all I can remember. I think it's something to do with the future. My future? I mean the feeling was like I was right on the edge, on the edge of the present and the past, like riding a breaking wave, and I was within one tiny fraction of a second of seeing into the future. Do you know what I mean?"

As she said it, she didn't really expect them to. She didn't even know herself.

The future, repeated Zoo slowly. "'We go into the future backwards.' A poet said that."

Eye shook her head. No, not backwards. Her eyes were wide open. And yet she could not recall what she had seen.

As silence began to drape the little kitchen again, the sun came out, and its rays pouring through the unwashed window picked out the grain of the wooden table, reflectively imprinted the window's pattern on the big jar of cereal, made the stopped antique clock on the far shelf gleam (its hands eternally pointing straight up to midday, or midnight), finally made golden the skin of the three women, so that they shone as one. After a suitable pause, then, Zoo moved her hand across the table to touch Eye's wrist lightly, her bangle too shining. "I will tell your fortune," she offered.

Eye said: "Susannah, I have to go to work." Also on the table was a box of tissues; she reached and pulled one out, wiping her face first with it and ending by blowing her nose and throwing it across the room to the overflowing lidless swing-bin, which it missed.

Dee, mug in one hand, dripping piece of toast in the other, chose this moment to leave the room, muttering something about "putting my face on".

Eye: Why did you say there may be four of us here?

Zoo thought for a moment; then she smiled. "It is one of those things that one says — without thinking too much. But now I remember, my grandmother — in Germany, when I was small — always laid a place at the table for 'the uninvited guest'."

Eye: The uninvited ghost?

Zoo: It's a similar word in German also.

A prickle in the spinal column, goosebumps on the skin. Again Eye paused, and began another tack.

Eye: Do you remember, Zoo, when you first came, and I couldn't understand your accent? I'm having difficulty remembering things, but I remember that. And why do I understand it so plainly now? And why don't I understand anything else?

Zoo: Understanding is not so important.

Eye: It depends how you mean, understanding. There is something I need to understand. But I don't even know what it is.

Zoo: You were talking of the future. Will you allow me to tell your future? To read your fortune? Come, let me do ziss.

Zoo left the kitchen, almost bumping into Dee in the doorway, make-up half applied to her eyes, who was returning her empty coffee mug. Dee gazed at Eye for several moments. Then she sat down at the table.

Dee: I mean it, kid. You don't look well enough to go to

work. I'll ring them up. C'mon, it must be ages since you took a sickie.

Eye (smiling weakly): Dee, I'm perfectly all right.

Dee: Zoo going to do your cards?

Eye: There really isn't time.

Dee: She's good, is Zoo. No charlatanry there, you know. She did me yesterday, and it wasn't a flattery job, quite spinechilling in fact. I mean, you know me, materialist that I am, but underneath it I'm as spooked as the next woman by that kind of thing. And it's your real women's lore, the genuine article, she comes from a line of German witches apparently, you with me?

Eye nodded, but she was looking out of the window, her chin supported by her right hand, elbow on the table.

Dee (conspiratorial whisper): I just wish she had a different taste in music. All that apocalyptic art-rock. (Aloud:) Still, can't have everything, and Susannah's a pretty talented lady. So what d'you reckon, you're still set on going to that stupid office of yours? It's up to you. But I tell you something, you haven't been yourself all week, ever since, well, there's no use going into all that again.

Dreamily, only half listening, Eye stared into the sunshine. Then she reached over for the glass jar and began to spoon cereal into a bowl. She went to the fridge for the milk. A six-pack of lager there, five occupants only, though, the sixth plastic collar empty. That was odd.

She knew that an end had approached, and therefore also a beginning. Nothing would be the same from this morning on. She turned with the milkbottle in her hand, and spotting the tissue that had fluttered to the floor bent over to pick it up and consign it properly to the dustbin. A crumpled can poked out of the lidless bin.

Zoo returned, frowning. "I have my cards but my book has vanished. Has anyone seen my Tarot book?"

Eye tried to answer. But her voice had not the strength to set the air around it vibrating. Therefore nobody heard it.

2: Start from zero

Eye's job was to sit all day in front of a VDU screen, entering text not of her own origination. But this morning she was restless. She sat contemplating the implacable green blink of the cursor, moving out from zero into the world of appearances and fading to zero again, each time in less than the space of a second; perhaps a hundred times a minute. Every keystroke, every character she typed was logged in the computer's memory. It haunted her with its equivocal presence/absence.

Although she had never thought about it much before, it now came upon her how strange a way it was to make a living. She fused her consciousness with this small pulse-being that ceased to be and remade itself moment by moment, and created out of this the illusion of permanent reproduction. The reproduction belonged, not to her, but to the company — which, in recompense, paid her so much each month. Though it was a recompense for the parts of her consciousness that it had taken from her, it wasn't, of course, much. Because they (the powers that ruled the company) weren't interested in her consciousness, so long as its borrowing contributed to production, or rather, reproduction.

All this Dee had once explained to her at great length, though Eye, in the trance-like state that had persisted since she awoke, did not presently recall it. Dee thought Eye was wasting her talents in this job. The fact of the matter was that Dee's material contribution to the household, as a result of being unemployed, was negligible. As for Zoo, her studies were supported solely by subvention from her family abroad. Therefore it fell to Eye to fund most of the household budget.

The office was right in the middle of the great city, on the other side of the sluggish metropolitan river. Plumes of steam rose from the city's heat spots; the heat emanated from shop windows, gratings and internal combustion engines, or simply from the concrete and brick of its buildings, warmed by the sun. Air temperature here was permanently a few degrees higher than in the surrounding suburbs and countryside, a measure of the city's collective entropy, or work transforming to heat. Thus, it seemed as though summer would never end. But inevitably autumn approached even this heat island. Dusty metropolitan trees began to shed leaves. The city shimmered slowly. Its buildings, densely packed, projected solidity, such as attracts and retains the confidence of markets. The deep winding canyon/streets remained intact, an abundance of sufficiency. Starlings and pigeons roosted above them. A breeze began to blow. All this was beyond Eye's ken. Little engagement was possible with this world of appearances.

Why did Eye insist on coming to work this morning, despite her sense of disorientation, her loss of memory since waking with the image of the satellite, despite Dee's kindly discouragement?

She thought perhaps sheer familiarity, the utter normality of the world of work, would trigger her back to mindfulness, would bring everything "flooding back" or "into focus", depending on which metaphor you chose. After all, and she was continually testing this, it wasn't as though she couldn't function. She remembered everybody's names as soon as she saw them again, she found her way unerringly through the city streets on her bicycle to the office, she had not forgotten how to use the wordprocessor. So what was wrong? It was just that everything was flat, as in a film set, merely the bare appearances there, sufficient for daily discourse, but without substance, without history behind them. And there was that unaccounted-for gap.

Was Eye scared at losing her past?

No, not scared. On the contrary, she'd found a lovely calm to be in the midst of. She was like the computer; she'd been switched off, so many megabytes of temporary memory wiped, but no damage done. No harm. The only thing was: whenever she started thinking about it, speculating on the blankness, then dread began to creep over her, for no reason, with no object. So long as she maintained her imperturbability she was OK, peaceful, no problem. Thought generated perspiration and goosebumps. Floating was all right. She gazed at the machine. Its blank screen and winking cursor, oblivion to appearance and back to oblivion, reproached her.

Eye came to, with a guilty start, and began typing again. Her movements were repetitive, her fingers a blur on the keyboard. Her eyes flicked back and forth to and from the copy-holder.

You could hear the air-conditioning hum, and someone clink coffee mugs. Light was slatted, because it poured in through blinds; it landed on a dishevelled and thirsty spider plant on a shelf, and caressed it.

Someone asked her, did she want a coffee. She failed to register the import of the utterance. Repetitive movement may in certain circumstances transform to dance, or transcendence, but that wasn't it. Something had happened, perhaps had been extinguished — but what? Conversely, when particles collide with very high velocity their kinetic energy can be used to form the masses of new particles. In other words, from the big to the small, a zoom, as in the movies of certain classic film directors, and then back again: the small units of energy constantly build larger units of meaning. Except she wasn't sharing this now.

What she was sharing was magic, in its strictest form. A colleague had called her, but she paid no attention.

I said, did you want some coffee, repeated the colleague, amused at her distraction. Eye swung round on her swivel chair, flustered with mild embarrassment, smiled her hurried thanks. The noise of the grey open-plan office swarmed up at her ears then.

What did she mean by magic? Static certainly clung to her skin; she could feel it crackle. She sensed that it had been building as she cycled in to work, alongside the heavy traffic, over the big river bridge, with flow. It made the wool of her trousers cling to the skin of her calves. Now it actually rebounded off the baffles.

But that wasn't the heart of it. If magic is the dark link between the world of appearances and the human world, then that comes closer to the brink of what Eye felt. As though something was ending, or something beginning. A thousand, a million different pieces of information assailed her on her journey in, in ways that she had never noticed before: the random scatter of light from a line of plastic rubbish sacks tweak-sealed at the side of the chain-link fencing; the sudden scent of mortality from the mouth of a shaded alleyway (from the momentary stink coming out of an alleyway it is possible to reconstruct a whole metropolis, and in an instant to destroy it again); the inexorable pull of the tide on the brown river as she crossed it; darkness pooled in the shop windows lit by a severe rhythm of fluorescent flicker (zero to fullness and back within the space of a moment — too quick to register consciously, too slow to ignore). But above all this a bright sky smiled upon her. Something happened. Had happened?

Zoo had once said you remembered everything that ever happened to you, from birth (and indeed pre-birth) onward, only you repressed all but a tiny fraction of it, which means put it away in a remote recess of your mind, because consciousness has to be selective. Otherwise you'd go crazy. It burns a path somewhere — intermittent or cursive? And ahead blankness? like a dark screen, un-invaded by memory's glowing characters? nothing there till you put it there? No, that's not right, she thought, the future's not like that. It isn't just blankness, it's all there somewhere, future and past and present; and she felt it was like her brain, wiped of memory, which is asymmetrical, that is, referring only to the past, was waiting to be nudged into awareness of the whole thing. Just an edge away. Nudged out of its onward equilibrium.

But she also felt as though within her something had been begun to happen, been created, pushed outward from zero.

The colleague, bringing a mug of the usual terrible coffee from the machine, demanded "a penny for them". The colleague was a kindly soul. She had worked for the company all her life since leaving school. For her, the company was like one of those big fish on the coral reef that from time to time allow the little fish which would otherwise be prey to enter their gaping mouths and pick their teeth clean. Needless to say, it was the little fish that she identified herself with.

Eye gave her a dreamy, apologetic smile; she couldn't keep her mind on the job this morning. It had been a bad night. Bad dreams. Must have been, said the colleague, indicating. Eye glanced back at the screen.

It was filled with garbage. Doodlings that her idling fingers had tapped, not noticing.

The sight of the meaningless sequential accumulation of characters (she suddenly saw they were meaningless, that is) snapped her back to attention. She really had to get on with her work before the supervisor came by. She would wipe it. The coffee smelt horrid, lurking smugly in her mug. She placed her fingers on the keyboard.

A moment later she recoiled in shock. A blinding force had discharged itself throughout her body, ripping excitedly through every neuron, flinging her instantly into a different space. She heard her colleague's cry of alarm. Something was wet and hot; it turned out to be splashes of the coffee from her suddenly overturned mug, the bulk of which had turned into a slow brown stain spreading tidelessly across the grey carpet.

Now work was definitely suspended. The colleague helped her out of the open-plan office, through the swing doors, down the anonymous passageway to the Ladies. She kept intoning feebly, I'm all right, but she wasn't. People loomed.

In the Ladies, she suddenly felt faint beside the cold white basin. She wanted to be sick, and was. The colleague, clucking amiably, fetched a wad of tissues to wipe her mouth. She had actually passed out, apparently.

What was it? An electric shock off the computer, the discharge of a static build-up? She couldn't remember it happening to anyone else in that office before.

You must be tired, suggested the colleague helpfully.

Tired, that was it.

She inspected her face in a mirror that was losing its silver even as it gained unwanted transparency. Oh god I do look terrible, she thought to herself, puffy eyes pasty complexion hair just anyhow, and the light in here (it was stark) just makes it look worse. She had looked at herself in the mirror before, she remembered. Last night. The same puffy eyes. Why was that? She couldn't remember.

From the tap she patted cold water onto her face; that felt better. But there was still something. It was this building that was bothering her, with its unearthly isolation, preventing the charge that had been building up in her from draining naturally away into the environment; maintaining a field of force that kept her pinned to an insufficiently rich dimensionality, excluding her present from its past and future, so that it was as though she was moving through a dark passage unable to see either where she had been or where she was going. She cupped her hands under the running tap and lifted them to her lips.

The colleague ordered her to remain there while she went to fetch someone qualified to help. It was absurd, Eye insisted again she was all right. The kindly woman mentioned the union's health and safety officer. He ought to be told. No, look, began Eye, but the colleague was gone.

Sliding, she sank slowly to the tiled floor. Here, it was good, and cool. Nobody to disturb her. Air-conditioning hummed.

After a few moments, she noticed that her shoulder bag was beside her. Evidently, the colleague must have thoughtfully brought it. Searching for some more tissues, she rummaged inside it. What were these unfamiliar objects?

A man's wallet. A chequebook.

The account name printed on each cheque was:

Mr John and Mrs Sonia Newman

A feeling of blank incomprehension gripped her, behind which was more than a hint of dread; the dread of profound meaninglessness. Worse than the contemplation of the meaningless characters she had generated on the screen. Yet there was nothing more orderly or ordinary, on the face of it, than these objects: in the black leather wallet a few crumpled banknotes, credit cards, driving licence, the picture of an unknown woman, a stranger; the names neatly printed on each cheque and a cumulative balance scribbled on each stub. The horror of it, she decided, came precisely from its ordinariness. The computer doodling was just chance. This had a purpose, but the purpose was unknown.

She noted that the branch of the bank at which the account was held was only a few streets away from this office building. Did the chequebook and wallet then belong to someone who worked here, and had they somehow accidentally got into her bag? But she knew at once that they did not and had not: it wasn't simply that the name was not familiar to her as anyone who worked for the company, the knowledge welled up from somewhere deep enough to be, almost literally, unfathomable. More than accidental, her possession of the objects was a sign. But of what?

Who were Mr and Mrs Newman?

Memory had failed Eye, because it was merciful.

Was it here, in the company washroom, that she began her journey? or was that journey's engendering, its gestation, hidden in the secret period before that?

•

Business at the bank was curving up to its midday peak. Eye, recovered from her trauma of the morning, and officially on her lunch hour, peered through the glass door. A small queue had already formed, but it seemed to be moving briskly.

She pushed the heavy door and went in. But there was a tickle at her heels.

She looked around. A small eager black dog had followed her into the bank. It trotted in hopefully, tail erect and wagging, eyes bright, pink tongue flopping through its teeth. She smiled. It stopped, pricking its ears. Then it took a decision to investigate this novel environment further. Eye glanced back out into the street. There was no sign of an owner. Nobody took any notice. She joined the end of the queue.

Quickly, she reached its head, and approaching an available cashier, who appeared reassuringly small and female in her niche, parked the wallet on the counter and showed her the chequebook and cheque guarantee card. Can you tell me how much we have in our account? was her query.

She'd rehearsed the words in her mind over and over again ever since she'd formulated the plan, an hour after discovering the wallet in her bag. But the word "our" had a hollow ring to it which bounced off the four walls of the bank and came back to her ears slightly out of phase, threatening to disrupt the bond she'd tried to establish between her own smile and the smile of the cashier. It was all right, though: the cashier, glancing at the relevant digits, was already punching out codes with one finger on the keyboard of her small console; her slender finger, slightly crooked, like the beak of a hen pecking quickly at what crumbs of nourishment there might be on the hard ground of the farmyard. The cashier frowned briefly at her screen, then scribbled something on a piece of paper which she pushed under the glass towards Eye.

It seemed an enormous sum.

Eye was drawing breath for her next decision when there was a commotion. She turned around to see.

The black dog had been spotted by several clients: it was in a squatting posture in a corner, near the back end of the automatic cash dispenser, its hind legs slightly splayed, a worried look (she fancied) in its eyes. From its anus was slowly emerging a thin yellowish brown tube that began to coil neatly on the polished floor.

Huge delight was the main response of the clients. A jovial fat man standing at the next cash window saw it as an opportunity to touch Eye.

"Take a butcher's at that!"

But a harassed young male bank official in shirtsleeves was already making for the dog, clapping his hands briskly and sternly.

"You could crack jokes about 'making a deposit'," jovially remarked the fat man.

"Why don't you crack one then?" suggested Eye, smiling sweetly (not quite at him).

Not knowing how to respond, and deciding therefore on an alternative strategy of appearing fatherly and knowledgeable, the fat man instead replied: "Did you ever hear of Sigmund Freud?" He pronounced it "Frood".

Eye (even more sweetly): No!

Now the dog, having finished its defecation, was busily/energetically scraping imaginary earth over its production with its hind feet. Meanwhile, the harassed young bank official's hapless barking was ignored. Ribaldry rippled through the bank.

Eye took the chained biro from its stand and wrote out a cheque. For the signature, she imitated as far as she could the scrawl on the cheque guarantee card.

The small cashier, trying in vain to suppress giggles while exchanging comment with her colleague at the next window, did not even give it a second glance. To Eye's relief, she didn't even notice that the imitated signature was that of the husband. That would have been a tricky one to get out of. How do you want the money, she asked, in a break from hilarity.

The sweating young bank clerk was chasing the dog round and round the bank. From time to time, it yelped. A helpful client held the glass door open, just in case. The young man uttered an oath and slowed down; so did the dog.

The dog, spotting Eye and perhaps recognising a comrade, trotted up to her, wagging its tail. The cashier was counting out banknotes. They seemed to inhabit two separate worlds. Because after all the fat man made no sense, money isn't shit — the discarded past of a lived moment — but an absence, an empty promise of the future, that very future whose bluff she wanted to call. The dog smiled; she could see its teeth wetten; the gesture called her to mindfulness once more. The future could no longer be postponed.

The harassed young bank employee: Is this your dog, madam?

Eye: No, I never saw it before in my life.

The fat man: I think he likes you.

Eye: Hello, old thing.

The dog: ???

And now at last the young man was able to make a successful grab for the dog's collar. Its forepaws barely touching the
floor, it was marched towards the held-open glass door to the
street. Spontaneous applause.

Eye stuffed the bulky wad of notes into the wallet, and the
wallet into her shoulder bag. As she left the bank in search of
her bicycle, the young man, his face grimacing and averted, was
commencing to scoop up the shit, using (to the fat man's
delight) a cash deposit envelope and a makeshift shovel that
was really a leaflet about available mortgages.

.

The national art gallery, a neo-classical edifice, dominated a
square in the grandest part of the city, near the seat of government. In the middle of the square towered a fluted column
(guarded by four immense black reclining lions frowning with
blank eyes) — atop which, absurdly delineated against racing
clouds, stood the simulacrum of a Hero, gazing contempla-
tively forever across at the seat of government. "Lofty" was
probably the word which was meant to spring to your mind.

But Eye, not contemplating the contemplator, was in the
gallery this afternoon, having tethered her bicycle to the railings outside.

The lunch hour was at least two hours old now, but she had
not been able to bring herself to return to work. Her colleagues
would no doubt be surmising that her "turn" of the morning
had unsettled her enough to make her take the rest of the day
off sick. In fact, she felt fine now.

It was too warm in the gallery. Grey/silver wallpaper, overhead strip lighting. When she moved on the black vinyl seating,
it squeaked. Not many people here this afternoon. A uniformed man circled slowly, hands behind his back. The mes-

sage was clear. Looking at the pictures was one thing, but spending an hour in just the one spot, well.

Undeterred, Eye gazed at the picture in front of her, which filled her vision, that is, it was no smaller than her concentration was precisely capable of framing.

A sombre painting. A purposeful woman in a pink frock with one breast exposed ran in from the left holding in front of her a stringless bow. The object of her quest was an unfortunate with the head of a small stag who was being mauled to death by three, no four hounds (they were variegated: white, tan to dark brown, but the dog accompanying the woman was black, with a red collar — it bore a strong resemblance to the dog at the bank, which is what drew Eye's attention to it in the first place). The wood was mysteriously dim, with stray light only piercing here and there to reverberate from a patch of undergrowth or from background water. Clouds massed ominously, but they had a silver lining.

She gazed at it for some considerable time.

When the uniformed man's back was turned (she thought he'd disapprove) Eye popped a handful of peanuts (for protein) into her mouth. She decided silently to dedicate the painting to Dee. It was a painting Dee would probably like, and would find much to draw elaborate superstructures of theory from.

The painting next to it was smaller, strange and very different.

A collage of three human faces was positioned above a similar collage of three animal heads.

On the left, and facing left in profile was a very old man with fine chiselled cheekbone, wispy grey pointy beard and red cap. In the middle, full face but with the eyes turned slightly away, was a middle-aged man with a face made squarer than it was by a full black beard. On the right, and facing right was a pale youth with a chunky nose and tightly curled light brown hair.

Immediately below and in front of them were the animals. Facing the same way as the old man was a long snouted wolf's head. The heavy head of a lion, about to bare its fangs, was in full face. Like those of the middle-aged man above it, its eyes looked slightly away, but in the opposite direction to the middle-aged man's. Facing right was a faithful looking dog, its pink tongue just protruding from its jaws.

Inscribed in the picture above this composition were the words:

EX PRAETERITO   NI FUTUR ACTIONE DETURPIT
PRAESENS PRUDENTIA AGIT

The small explanation at the side translated this as "from the past...the man of the present acts prudently...so as not to imperil the future." This hideous conglomerate six-head could be an admonition, Eye thought. She screwed up her eyes to see whether she could superimpose the image of Zoo onto the black-bearded man in the centre, who would seem to be in the thick of it. It was possible, though a difficult feat of the imagination. But there was no question about the dedication this time: this was Zoo's picture, Eye decided.

And (allowing for the sexism of the translated Renaissance language) she accepted the admonition in the text as a Sibylline utterance of Zoo's.

Turning round to look over the seat's back, she scanned now the third picture, which she had earlier examined cursorily.

Not only was it bigger than the other two, but it glowed twice as brightly with life and colour.

At the extreme left, in off-the-shoulder copper sulphate blue and scarlet robes, a solitary woman trod the beach. She was surprised by a naked youth manipulating a billowing pink rag who leapt at her, suspended in the middle of the picture's air, from a two-wheeled cart hauled by two placid cheetahs. Accompanying the youth and emerging from the thicket at the right were a band of half-nude revellers, including: a muscular bearded man whose thigh, waist and arm were entwined in snakes; another man with furry thighs and a modest belt of leaves, brandishing the torn-off haunch of an animal (possibly that of the deer whose severed head lay mournfully on the ground); a plump woman clashing cymbals; and a chubby child-satyr strutting with some silk on his shoulder. The chubby satyr (Eye now noticed, with pleasurable recognition) was being reproached by a small black dog. In the "distance" the smoke-blue of the mountains descended into the aquamarine of the sea, and in the sky above the clouds, way above the solitary woman's head twinkled a crown of eight stars.

This magnificent picture, whose colours leaped out with the same worrying loveliness as that of the youth in its centre, was surely none other than her own.

Pleased with the symmetry she had construed, Eye became aware of the miserable woman only when she started muttering.

The miserable woman had sat down unobtrusively beside her, emerging slowly and unseen at first from the background. For all Eye knew, she might have escaped from another painting. The strip lighting laid a ghastly sheen on her hair which was a nondescript colour and smoothed away either side of a centre parting before becoming straggly at her thin neck, while her beige jumper below the shiny-with-use anorak had turned livid. What she was staring at in her hand as she muttered was a small book. Now Eye got a good look at her, but turned away politely or in embarrassment. Watery-blue yet intense eyes is what she saw.

The miserable woman spoke. "I come over all funny in there, I had to come away. I had to say a prayer, all them books about War." She stopped, to indicate it was Eye's turn.

Sticking to the obvious, Eye asked, "In where?" The book, she saw, was a bible with tattered black covers, some yellowed pages loosened from their binding.

The woman: Yeah, over there, the bookshop.

Eye: D'you mean the gallery bookshop, or one of the book-shops outside?

The woman: ???

Eye (now wishing she'd not taken up the challenge of the conversation): Which bookshop? There are quite a few book-shops around.

The woman read from her tract for a moment, almost silently but her lips moving. Then she looked up. She considered.

"Yes, there are quite a few bookshops," she repeated rather slowly, then continued to mouth dumbly after the sentence had finished, as though this were some new and devastating piece of information.

Eye offered the miserable woman her bag of peanuts. The miserable woman shook her head sadly. Was she sad? She looked sad; no, not sad, more as though an ancient tragedy had entered her life at least ten years ago and had yet to leave it. Eye shrugged, and put another handful in her mouth; she needed the protein after all she'd been through. And all she was yet to go through? But that was blurred; it didn't yet make sense; it was the unknown. The last thing she needed now was fear, and it was fear that she saw in the woman's eyes, not fear of War as she had at first thought, but (an important modification) fear of books about War, in other words be silent about it and it doesn't exist — which was bad magic, Eye thought. She suppressed a wry smile when she looked back up at the painting she had last been contemplating and saw the sixfold head, which didn't seem so hideous now, superimposed in her imagination by an image of the three See No Evil Hear No Evil Speak No Evil monkeys. Now she turned back to the woman, who began to look like a frightened monkey. Was it possible that she was right to fear the accumulation of information about the horror, rather than the horror itself? (The woman was now praying again, reading/muttering from her tract, oblivious to Eye's wonder. The uniformed man circled more tightly, suspicious.)

Aloud, Eye said: "I've been looking at these three pictures for the past hour. What do you think of them?"

The woman, startled, looked up. She looked blank at first, then, slowly, gazed at each painting in turn. The island where the naked Bacchic figure had created a crown of stars in the blue sky for the solitary woman on the beach. The virgin huntress with her dogs, having her revenge. The mysterious collage of human and animal heads, looking into the past, present and future. Finally, she said in a low whisper, not looking at Eye:

"Holy, holy, holy."

Perhaps there was another way of looking at it, perhaps the information acted as a sort of positive feedback, actually intensifying the horror. Therefore the city was a focus, an accumulator, and anyone in it was vulnerable. So what did the paintings represent to the miserable woman? Holy, holy, holy. What kind of exegesis was this? Did she mean "holy" to be applied to each in turn? In what way did they plant the idea of sacredness in her head? Could they be divinatory in any way, that is, pointing to an outcome of the present predicament, whatever that was? These questions were important, because Eye had got to the point where she needed to finalise plans for her next move. Clearly, she wasn't going back to work now; the afternoon was far advanced in its march towards no return.

But the miserable woman offered no solution. And suddenly, Eye began to hate her.

She hated her because of her shiny thin hair and her worn-out anorak and her livid jumper and her shapeless skirt. She hated her for her sad watery eyes, and the way her thin lips trembled as her eyes moved over her text. She hated her for the plastic supermarket carrier bags she now saw rested at her feet, bulging with useless things. She hated her therefore for her homelessness, and her rootlessness.

This wouldn't do. Eye got up, dreadfully agitated, walked around a bit pretending to look at the pictures again. She hated the miserable woman because she was weak, she was marginal, because she had given up, because she was a victim, and victims deserved to be hated. She almost burst into tears at the thought of such hate and its unfairness.

•

Now it was early evening. Eye walked slowly wheeling her bicycle along the south bank of the metropolitan river, moving westward, so that the yellow glow deposited on low cloud by the hidden sun was directly in front of her eyes. The city authorities had placed "gas lamps" at regular intervals along the embankment; they were period imitations, not of course really powered by gas, and the germ of electricity was now beginning to grow from nothingness in each one. In addition, red and white fairy lights had been strung up prettily in repeated swags.

To her left was a vast concrete building that also began to shimmer with lights — a famous concert hall — in front of whose wide glass doors people milled, dressed smartly for an occasion they had anticipated with polite happiness. To her right the sluggish water of the river moved past her beyond the exposed mudflats whereon a quantity of seabirds pecked and ate ravenously. On the water itself more seabirds swam, or rather floated pacifically, wings folded, about a hundred of them she thought, souls of dead sailors they say, spaced evenly out so that they didn't interfere with each other. And they were grey in the less than good light here. But on the far bank, more illuminated buildings and high cranes, static now.

And there was music coming from somewhere. She stopped, leaning on the parapet to watch the water: its greyness was flecked with yellow-gold that the sky had given it. Further ahead was a dark railway bridge which without warning thundered in response to its momentary bright load, a suburban multiple-unit electric train taking the last of the commuters from the terminus on the north side of the river to their dispersed and welcoming homes beyond the southern limits of the city. No doubt one or two of those trains would contain some of her colleagues from the office, their day done.

She had made her mind up shortly after leaving the art gallery. On a street corner just off the classical square dominated by the stern Hero on his sky-high pedestal was a post office. She had purchased a stamp, then finding a crumpled envelope in the bottom of her shoulder bag had taken the wad of banknotes from the man's wallet, divided it in half and put half the money in the envelope. She had licked it sealed; had written on the front the names of Dee and Zoo and the address of the house; posted it.

The other half of the wad she had concealed about herself; more specifically, she had momentarily loosened her woollen trousers and stuffed it down the front of her knickers. Then she'd retrieved the bicycle, tethered to the railings outside the art gallery.

She had cycled through the city streets. Before long, the light was starting to fade; traffic beginning to thicken again for the evening rush. Once, she had heard a high harsh sound above the boom of the traffic; turning a corner, she'd found the cause: above a square lined with garish cinemas the sky was black with thousands of starlings that clouded above a massive tree, screaming to each other.

Now she leaned on the parapet. And the water was silent as it poured towards the distant estuary.

Under the railway bridge appeared an approaching tug-boat hauling downriver its train of dark barges piled with rubble. It passed her, moving majestically.

The grey bridge was outlined in reddish hues fading upward to a dull orange and then to mauve and indigo; it was wonderful. A star or two might now pierce this multi-hued veil, she thought, gazing intently, hoping for a glimpse of such unknown entities — the Pleiades, the Hunter, the Twins — that might be permitted to penetrate the city's generated pall. It was a rare night sky that was thus populated in this polluting metropolis. But there was a bright point. Which vanished when she looked straight at it and seemed to reappear as soon as she looked slightly away. It was directly over the distant railway terminus. "The evening star," she said to herself.

The unthinkable entered her mind and frightened her. All at once her euphoria dissipated again, and dread took its place, which could not be escaped. Was it the evening star? Was it falling? Once or twice she felt that it was she who was falling — upward? — towards it. The third time she tried to recreate the sensation she failed, perhaps because she was distracted by a gust of breeze that without warning came whipping at her from the direction of the bridge, cancelling her concentration with the suddenly enhanced sound of that music — apparently a solo violin.

SATELLITE TO CRASH TOMORROW? shrieked the headline on a poster for the evening paper.

With a small passing shiver that had nothing to do with the breeze, she wheeled her bike on. Crowds in smart coats thickened. The auditorium inside the big concrete and glass concert hall would be filling up now, but that wasn't where the music was coming from. No: as she got nearer she saw that it was a bearded busker at the foot of a flight of steps close to the railway bridge over the river. Despite his dishevelled appearance — the beard was a straggle of interspersed grey, his blue anorak was almost the same grey in parts and, as the miserable woman's had been, shiny with wear, while dried mud clung to his boots — he dispersed notes in a surprisingly orderly, stately yet graceful, fashion. At his feet on the tarmac coins glistened/nestled in a small black upturned beret. She thought the music was by Bach, at least that was a name that sprang to mind. But stopping, she became entranced; she leaned the bike once more against the parapet; she didn't know quite what to do about her body language. Bach was speaking, or was he singing, through this man's muscles through his vibrating beard through his vibrating violin. She looked up again at the white point of the evening star that could be the satellite, solitary above the gloom where the railway terminus would be, on the far side of the river. Was it the satellite? perhaps not yet. She wanted to smile. Instead, she closed her eyes. Now the music was coming from nowhere, purest generation out of nothing, but it was moving surely into the future, opening up the future. Without words, it was describing the future, which is where she wanted to be. Dread lay in the locked past, only in the future was there hope of more than a margin for survival, and the music, the Bach or whatever, was surely taking her there. It came out liquid, not like out of a tap, but as though a rock, the hard rock of the past, had been pierced, and it emerged, gushed from the dark secret place, streamed; it forked here and there and divided itself into parts, the parts having independent existence, but hearing each other's chiming and remaining in rough synchrony, waiting to merge again, see, it all really made sense after all, it was the one stream that had pretended to be several streams, it was only kidding. And the sound itself sometimes was a narrow sound, thin and brittle, as if it was in danger of snapping off into silence, and then it became thicker, more mellifluous, more resonant, bouncing off the concrete that she knew was there, before resuming its slenderness and becoming slow. The slowness was the actual future, awesome but full of light. Several people descended the steps during this charmed period; she could hear them, mostly in couples or small groups, she guessed, making for the concert hall, and most would not even be looking at the busker. But when she opened her eyes again she saw one of them drop a coin in his beret causing his eyebrows to quiver subtly in acknowledgement. While she'd been plunging into heaven the darkness had gathered fast.

There were brighter lights than ever on this bright bank.

Were the seabirds still out there? yes, asleep on the waters. A motor launch, lit up, was coming the other way (upstream).

The bridge, overhead now, roared again, almost overhauling the music but not quite.

Now the music came to an end.

The man went down on his haunches to read some sheet music he had taken from his bag, which he was obviously having difficulty seeing properly, because he was some way from the nearest fake-gas-lamp standard. He held his violin by the neck, like a slim dead chicken, its tail resting lightly on the tarmac, the bow clasped to it in the same hand. She fumbled with the front of her trousers.

Out came the thick bundle of notes at last. Selecting one, which though of the least denomination in the wad was still too much, she came forward and tossed it in the man's beret. But even at that small distance it fluttered away in the wrong direction, so she had to grab at it again, and this time place it, gently.

The man's eyebrows did a few flutters. Straightening up, he bowed formally, as though he were not a busker under the bridge at all, but on stage in the concert hall across the concourse. "Thank you," smiled his eyes.

She smiled back now. Retreating, she said: "For the souls of dead sailors."

"Why not?" said the man's eyes, then with one movement replacing the instrument on his chin he commenced a salty, jig-like tune.

"Goodbye," she said.

Shouldering the bicycle with some difficulty, she began to mount the steps. It appeared that they led up to a walkway which hugged the side of the railway bridge across the river. So now she was heading back towards the north bank, the wind really quite chilly. She wheeled the bike in and out of oncoming groups of people who were crossing the bridge in the opposite direction, making for the concert hall. She had been on this narrow pedestrian bridge before. She hated its precariousness; the way you could glimpse water between the slats.

Halfway across, she stopped. The water far below all black and shiny as it moved. And further out gold where it caught the lights, the mudflats reflecting gold/fuzzy the lights of the big concert hall now to her right as she looked out and the water reflecting them gold/wobbly. But where were the seabirds? The souls of dead sailors? Now she couldn't see any sign of them. As though they had magically vanished with the coming of dusk. Was that possible?

Something was not comfortable, something kind of slow-burned in her mind. She groped in her shoulder bag. The wallet, the cheque-book. The photograph of the woman. She drew them out. They were hot with something like pain; she gazed wonderingly, but still, though something tugged at her memory, she could not figure out where they had come from, or who

Mr John and Mrs Sonia Newman

were. Was that really her in the creased photograph? However, now it was time to say goodbye. She leaned over the railing. It made her sick with dizziness to do so. Perhaps some of the pedestrians on the walkway looked at her oddly as they passed, or with some concern or apprehension, but she didn't care about that.

She dropped the cheque-book, and the wallet and photo after it, into the river.

She wanted to hear the double splash as they hit the water seconds later. In this, she was disappointed, for just at that moment the bridge had begun to shiver as though in ecstasy and immediately a bass rumble swelled to enormous magnitude as another train passed by on the main bridge above and just behind her back. The sound of the cheque-book and wallet hitting the water was therefore too faint to carry above this; but she thought she saw them enter, and the water close about them. Looking down this way increased her dizziness. Looking up at the sky, then, she noted its darkness, devoid of heavenly bodies. No sign even of that point of light she had momentarily construed as the satellite plunging earthwards.

She reached the other side of the river.

On firm ground again beside the railway terminus she re-mounted her bike. Energy was beginning to flood through her — adrenalin? — reaching peak level suddenly. There before her were beautiful shops still open, full of wool and magazines and cameras and wine, and warm inviting restaurants: a flow of commerce that showed no sign of dying down. The future still beckoned.

Eye thought she would cycle around the centre of the city for a while. Despite the welcoming appearance of this commerce, she knew it could be dangerous if she stopped. But so long as she remained on her magical protective bicycle she would be filled with the adrenalin, if that is what it was, which would ward off any possible evil from such commerce, keep it glued to its position as though self-charmed by its own hypnotic power. The bicycle generated good power, a field of force that repelled bad commerce. She steered out from the side street onto the main thoroughfare where buses, taxis and cars roared into the endless, approaching night.

•

Magic. The link between the world of appearances and the human form. It was mediated by Eye's bicycle, which shone with it. She loved her bicycle, and could easily have composed verses in celebration of it. When she rode it through the city streets that evening, she no longer felt powerless; it was a gleaming charger, an angel-cradle.

Handlebars, bell, gear lever, front and rear lamps, forks, frame, saddle, saddle-bags, wheels, mudguards, chain, pedals: all shone with the magic of transformation.

She had not returned to work, and she had decided she wasn't going back home either. Not this evening. If the past was a source of unnamed horror, then only the future offered hope. She had to trust to the future.

Remembering she had only had a bag of peanuts to eat since breakfast, she bought a hamburger at a stall, and sat down to eat it on a bench in a small public space thronged by tourists, her bicycle tethered next to her. But she wasn't really hungry, and ended up sharing it out to the pigeons and sparrows who still foraged even at this late hour.

She bought a bottle of orange juice and stowed it in her saddle-bag.

She rode the bicycle round and round the crowded streets of the theatre district.

She stopped at a public call-box, got off, and tried to make a call. The ringing tone persisted for some time, but nobody answered.

Money crackled sweetly in her crotch.

While she was at the call-box, a man with a glass eye came up to her and started making feeble jokes — reminding her of the fat man in the bank at noon. Deliberately, she rolled her head and her eyes round and round, making strange crazy noises in her chest. He soon got the message and made off.

This part of the city teetered on the edge of civilisation. The bicycle took her to a dark alleyway under another bridge, which stank of urine and human sweat. It was as though someone had abruptly switched the lights off. Dimly, she could see a figure moving slowly, weighed down with bags. It reminded her of the miserable woman in the art gallery.

The sight filled her with remorse. The magic vanished instantly. She thought of how she'd left the miserable woman, just got up in the middle of a conversation, hands clenched, and walked away. How rude the woman must have thought her, but it was just the force of emotion at that very moment, she hadn't really meant anything by it. She wanted to tell the woman this now, she wanted to apologise. She stopped the bicycle and dismounted. Hello, she called to the dark figure. But of course it wasn't the miserable woman at all; in fact it was a man with a dark face. As he came into a patch of light she saw that he was wizened, he had a mischievous look in his eye, and he wore a sort of kilt of blanket material over his ragged trousers and trainers. Another blanket was draped over his shoulders, and on this were pinned countless badges and military style medals, assorted birds' feathers and other trinkets. Round his neck were chains from which more feathers were suspended as pendants, and several necklaces, some of fake pearls, some of shells, some of coins. More coins had been fastened to his forehead by some means which Eye couldn't figure out, and he wore a beret on his head covered with badges. One arm was covered in bangles, the other in an array of cheap wristwatches.

He put his weighty bags down and touched her on the arm. He grinned. "You got any spare change, young miss?" he said, winking and bobbing up and down.

Eye: Yes, of course.

She fumbled inside her trousers and came up with some banknotes. She pressed one into the man's outstretched, grimy hand. He continued to bob up and down, combining this rapid vertical motion with a slower bowing from the waist, while touching the note to the coins plastered on his forehead. It was a complicated and subtle dance.

Eye: I mistook you for someone else. I was looking for a woman.

The man: Oh, I ain't no woman, young miss. I'm the Spice

Man. Hey (pointing to the bicycle), that's a fine machine you got there.

Eye (sudden smile): It's magic.

The Spice Man: Yeah, seen. A machine got to be live and intelligent, then you can put your mind into it, know what I mean?

Eye: Do you know the woman I'm looking for? She's got grey hair and wears an anorak and a beige jumper, and she reads from the bible. I need to apologise to her.

The Spice Man: There ain't no need to apologise. The bible is in your head. You know? It's in your head. Jesus is your brain and the Devil is your wits. That's the truth. It's the living truth, but you need the machine to send it out. You got a good machine.

Eye: I'm afraid I might have offended her, but I didn't mean to.

Another figure emerged from the shadows, a young man with spiky hair, a cigarette end glowing in his hand. Although the evening had whipped up a chill, he wore nothing over his ripped tee-shirt. He clapped the Spice Man genially on the shoulder. "Hey Spice, you giving this lady hassle?"

The Spice Man: No, man.

Eye handed another banknote to the young man. "I'm looking for a woman, I think she may be homeless. She's got two plastic carrier bags full of stuff and talks out loud to herself."

The young man: Oh, cheers. Well, that really narrows it down, dunnit?

Eye: She reads the bible and she has grey hair and wears an anorak.

The young man: Hmm. Could be Rita.

The Spice Man: No man, it's Ellen.

The young man (making a face and gesturing at Eye to indicate "off his head"): What you talking about, Ellen works on the soup run.

Eye: Well, if it is Rita, tell her from me I'm sorry I didn't say goodbye, but my mind's on other things. I met her at the art gallery, I'm Eye.

The Spice Man: Ah, right on. I and I climb a mountain.

The young man (waving his cigarette butt languidly): Yeah, sure. Hey, you look as if you're in the money.

He pointed at the sheaf of banknotes in her hand.

Eye: I was lucky today. D'you have mates, there, sleeping?

The young man: Yeah.

She saw bodies inertly reclining under the bridge, each within masses of newspaper and dearly prized cardboard boxes. Although darkness had only recently fallen, many were soundly asleep and had obviously been so for some time. There was a powerful human smell. She went from one to another, wheeling the bike as she moved; at each she stooped, unpeeled a banknote from the wad, and tucked it under the makeshift covers with a whispered "Good luck". There was no reaction from most, but one or two sat up in puzzlement. The young man accompanied her, making appropriate comments, such as "Oh well, you needn't bother with him, he's well out of it", while the Spice Man, bags assumed anew, recommended his bobbing and now handicapped dance.

One man, not that old but indescribably ragged, stood up, gesticulated. He came after her, speaking, but his words made no sense. The more clearly she heard them the less sense they made. It was no language she had ever heard, light years beyond even the Spice Man's discourse. He put a hand on her handlebar; his breath smelt heavily of booze. The young man, self-appointed as Eye's protector, restrained him.

She'd come to the end of the line. There was no sign of the miserable woman after all. She shook hands with the young man and the Spice Man, realising now the uselessness of her quixotic action, distributing alms like the Lady Bountiful. Stupid uselessness. But perhaps it wasn't meant to have a use, in that sense. Perhaps it was about establishing links and boundaries. The links went with the boundaries. There was something that bound her even to that senseless, homeless man, who was now being chaperoned away by the young man and the Spice Man, and at the same time there was a gulf, an empty galactic space between his language and hers. His hand had brushed hers as it gestured at the handlebars; it felt dry, like paper, as though there was nothing behind it. In a sense, there wasn't. There was no past here under the bridge and certainly no future, just the husk that formed around the immediate present, but nobody cared.

I have to go, she said, getting on the bicycle again, I'm sorry. Three figures, one tottering, one bobbing and one waving a cigarette butt. The bridge roared.

The bicycle took her to some smart shops, which were still open at this hour for the tourist trade. Guiltily, she bought a blue silk scarf at one, which she put round her head after the fashion of an Arab woman.

She felt cold. No need to. She had money, hadn't she? She went into the adjoining shop and selected a coat of dark, ribbed wool, almost the most expensive in the shop. She tried it on before a full-length mirror. Just the job. The assistant gave her a snooty look. Perhaps she smelt the remnants of homelessness on her.

At a stationer's, she craved a black notebook with a red spine. The pages were cream, and lined in faint turquoise, the endpapers mottled turquoise, with a picture of a flying eagle on the back and MADE IN CHINA. She would use it to write down her future dreams. She noticed that, although summer was barely over, some Christmas merchandise was already on display. She bought a small tube of pulverised tinsel, or glitter. Magic dust. It gave her child-like pleasure.

If the bicycle could have smiled, it would have.

•

Something was wrong, though. The bicycle magic had concealed this for a while, but she now became aware that the city was in terrible danger.

It was not clear why until she returned to the grand square presided over by the Hero on his high pedestal. It was still thronged with buses and tourists, but the art gallery which brooded over one side of the square was now closed for the night. Here, she could look up and see a fair expanse of evening sky for a change. Starless. The pall which enveloped most of the city was broken only in two places, lighter patches, one the milky swaddling round the concealed moon, and in the centre of the other a point of light, the same point of light she'd seen earlier, from the other side of the river, twinkling over the railway terminus. The same now-you-see-me-now-you-don't quality. Whenever she looked directly at it, it seemed to disappear, only to re-enter her field of vision as she directed her gaze slightly away. It surely was the descending satellite.

On news-stands all over the centre of the city, the same headline had been displayed:

SATELLITE TO CRASH TOMORROW?

She wished now she had bought a paper to read today's update on the story. Yet she knew at the same time it would not have told her the truth. If there was any chance the satellite might fall on the city, it would have been certain that *they* (she couldn't analyse the word any further, or gloss it as anything more precise than *the powers*) would not have released this information. Therefore buying the paper would not have achieved anything, in fact it would have actively clouded her understanding, if anything.

Was that the key to the miserable woman's fear of books about war?

Eye had dismounted, and was on the pavement, directly facing the monument, the stone lions and the fountains, which played softly golden in the floodlights. A few tourists wandered beside them, and still the pigeons pecked their way between. Near her, a public call-box. She tried again. At the other end of the line, the phone just went on ringing. No answer. She put the receiver down, and her coins tumbled back into her possession.

She now noticed with a thrill of fear that some of the big buildings surrounding the square had devices on their roofs, some kind of electronic surveillance equipment, including what looked like satellite dishes. What if it was this that was attracting the dying satellite? What if the power, or the powers, were unwittingly inviting their own nemesis? But it would not be just the powers that would be destroyed. The city would suffer cataclysmic devastation. Millions of people would die. The busker, the miserable woman, the homeless people sleeping under the bridge, Dee and Zoo snug in their house and Eye herself on her magic bicycle — they would all be swallowed up in the disaster, they would be insignificant among the statistics if this came to pass.

Ahead, on the other side of the square, was an immense stone triumphal arch, with carved statuary in its niches, and a full complement of raised coats of arms. It was joined to the buildings on either side, and was actually a building itself, because windows were embedded in it, too.

Flags hung limply in the night air, illuminated.

Below a Latin inscription, three immense openings, two for pedestrians and one for traffic, revealed the roadway beyond.

Eye remounted her bicycle. Launching herself into the stream of traffic, which was less thick than it had been earlier in the evening, she held her right arm out to get to the other side. Now she was in the correct lane to approach the great arch. Lights changed from red to red-amber to green; she darted past the emerald like a greyhound from its trap, furiously pumping.

Beyond the arch the roadway was wide, and illuminated at frequent intervals by high, powerful lamps. The tarmac revealed by this lighting was not the dark grey of the rest of the city's streets, but had a pinkish hue, lending it the appearance of a mile-long red carpet that had been unrolled from the arch to its distant objective. Eye's tyres made a low and pleasant sizzle on it as she pedalled.

On the right hand side was a row of elegantly classical buildings. On the left, a flat park with trees. Portable metal barriers were stacked by the side of the road, waiting for the crowds they were intended to fence in. But there were no crowds at this time of night.

The more she pedalled the more Eye's foreboding grew.

The city was an accumulator of bad energy, and she was approaching the heart of it. The energy was a homing beacon for the satellite. A terrible disaster was in prospect.

Eye saw the bright spark become an unbearable radiance, a midnight sun that could not be resisted. The whole of the metropolis shared its ghastly light for a few paralysed moments. And then horror on a grand scale: buildings toppling, the ground lifting away, dust veiling the shrieking men, women and children. Finally, the firestorms racing through the city, whipped by a terrible wind....

As the satellite approached the city (and there was no evidence to contradict this), so Eye approached the end of the long straight road. A vast monument of complicated construction marked the culminating point; and beyond, after an open space, a large sprawling grey building, many of its windows aglow, well secluded behind a courtyard surrounded by iron railings.

The royal palace was at the very heart of the city. In fact, Eye had a strong feeling, as she pedalled round the monument to a past monarch, that it *was* the heart; she felt its palpable beat, a message radiating not only horizontally to the metropolis around, but out into the blackness of the air above. It was the origin of the homing beacon which could bring the doomed satellite hurtling down towards a catastrophe.

Although frightened, she did not cease her pedalling, nor even falter, but turned left on her magic bicycle and selected the road that skirted the left hand side of the palace.

Beyond the iron railings, in the courtyard, she could see soldiers stock-still on guard, and one or two policemen. Little traffic passed her on the road, other than an occasional taxi. During the day, this area would be teeming with tourists, but they had all gone.

She was overwhelmed by the idea that it was up to her to take protective measures. Why? She didn't know. Maybe in daylight things would have appeared different. But a line from a poem surfaced again and again into her consciousness:

Weave a circle round him thrice …

The palace was slipping out of view. It seemed from the corner of her eye to shine with an uncanny, perhaps unsavoury glow.

She was re-entering a built-up area: big offices. At the next available right turn, she found herself on a main thoroughfare where the traffic was fast. She kept as much to the side of the road as she could. Suddenly, she felt something in her pocket. Of course — it was the tube of glitter dust. Some prevision must have caused her to buy it. Without disturbing her rhythm, she drew it out one-handed, and with a finger prised the top until it flew off to drop behind her into the road. Then, as she began manoeuvring to get in the right position for an approach to a major road junction, she worked the tube until it was held against the handlebars at just the right angle. Tiny amounts of the dust began to spill, making a narrow, intermittent and almost invisible silver trail. She had to be careful not to overtip it, otherwise too much of the dust would spill at once. When she had to stop at a red light, she kept the tube upright.

Round a terrifying traffic intersection she went. It required the utmost concentration, laying the trail, steering the bike and signalling her intention to turn against the traffic flow, all at the same time.

Now she left the traffic and the buildings, and was once more on a tree-lined avenue. With luck, she would have done a complete circuit of the royal palace. She was proved right: she was approaching the monument in front of the palace, from a different direction this time.

She sped past the palace. Once, she looked up into the sky, but could see only blackness.

She was back with the traffic. The question was: would she pick up the beginning of her silver trail? Would the dust last out?

She remembered the traffic sign she'd passed just at the point where she'd started the trail. Of course, the trail itself was too faint to be visible. Seconds later, she realised the tube was empty. Just in time. It had lasted long enough to complete the magic circle.

Two more circuits of the palace now. First, the terrifying traffic intersection, then the tree-lined avenue, then the monument up ahead....

On her third approach to the monument, chaos broke out.

First, she heard a banshee siren behind her, which swelled rapidly in volume until it was unbearable. Then there was a swirl of white, blue flashing lights, red, and a screech of brakes.

A police car hugged her vision. From it, an official arm was waving her down. Her heart in her mouth, she realised she would have to pull over.

Now there were two police cars. They were white, with orange flashes. And a motorcycle pulled up. She was in the midst of uniformed officers. One of them was talking into a radio on his lapel. The motorcycle seemed to be keeping up a raspy, trebly radio conversation with itself, without the need for human intervention. "Papa delta, can you assist with the lost boys, er, small lesbian, er, something approaching north-west, over," it said. But nobody did anything about it.

Another siren swelled up out of the night and yet another vehicle, a police van, screeched to a halt alongside.

She got off her bike and started to tremble as they surrounded her.

The gaiety of the lights and the noise resembled that of a small circus that had just pitched its tents by the side of the road.

A large officer with sad eyes confronted her. Where was she going, he asked her, in a voice pregnant with gentleness. It seemed like he really did want to know.

But Eye's voice was once again affected by the feebleness she had experienced that morning, at breakfast, when Zoo had been searching vainly for her Tarot book. It started well enough in her chest, but before long got hopelessly lost in a labyrinth somewhere in her throat. So she just stood there, looking at the blue light flashing on and off her hands gripping the handlebars, then looking back at the policeman. The good, kind policeman.

"Come on, love, nobody's going to hurt you," he was wheedling. Suddenly he was the father she would like to have had. But not for long. Another officer, weasel-like and abrupt, butted in.

"What are you doing here?" he demanded.

Still she could not reply.

The bad, weasel-like policeman: OK, just freeze.

He motioned to a policewoman who emerged from the shadows. (There were about twelve figures around.)

The good policeman (laying firm white hands on her bicycle): I'll hold onto this.

The policewoman took her firmly by the shoulder and led her under a street lamp. She began patting Eye up and down. She dug her hands in Eye's pockets.

Eye heard the good policeman and the bad policeman conferring over the objects from her pocket. "It's tinsel stuff," she heard the bad policeman say in a perplexed mutter as he turned the tube over and over. A third policeman was going through her shoulder bag and her saddlebag. Withdrawing the Chinese notebook she had bought at the stationer's, he was going through it page by page, not trusting its utter blankness. A fourth policeman searched the grassy kerb with a torch.

The policewoman was now shining another torch into her mouth. "Open wider," she was saying, like a dentist. Eye remembered to her horror the wad of banknotes stuffed in her knickers, and her heart skipped. She would never be able to explain that amount of money. But fortunately the policewoman's search was not quite that intimate.

"System six, castration, er oriental trappings, over," the motorcycle radio was going.

The bad policeman returned. He handed the objects from Eye's pockets back to the policewoman "Name," he snapped.

"You'll have to answer," the good policeman told her sadly.

Eye thought. Then she said clearly:

"Mrs Sonia Newman."

The name dropped into a little silence like a bottomless puddle. During this silence, Eye's heart did not beat at all.

Then the bad policeman said: "Date of birth."

Eye found half to her own surprise that she remembered her date of birth. She told him.

The bad policeman conferred with the man with the radio. The good policeman continued to look sad, and held onto her bike. The policewoman pretended to be a zombie. They were all like people trapped into abstractions, not like animals on a planet; they were unheeding of the wide sky above them. As though random numbers had been allotted them, and they with no choice in the matter, a definition of tragedy maybe, except that there would be no loopholes through which they might escape, and therefore no suspense or anything that might pass for thought. That was both frightening and comic, thought Eye. What would Dee make of it? Probably a long and incoherent speech.

Long minutes went by. Then without warning, her bicycle and possessions were thrust back into her hands.

The bad policeman confronted her.

The bad policeman (almost spitting): OK, I want you out of here.

The good policeman (sternly): You don't want to stay around, it's not a good idea. At the end of the day, it really is very late in the day.

The van and one of the cars revved up simultaneously and hysterically and vanished in a flash of confusing lights.

Eye: But it's all right, the satellite's not going to crash, not here. Not now.

The bad policeman: Just get going, please.

Eye remounted her bike in enormous relief, feeling the money crackling in her crotch as she did so. She was amazed that nobody heard this, or at least gave any sign of doing so. The policewoman retreated; meanwhile the motorbike, its radio still chattering, swelled its engine importantly and prepared to move off. "Slag one-two, just a dog, excessively flowery, over," it snapped, with evident disappointment.

Shakily, she pedalled into the road. Behind her the remaining car and the motorbike prowled, and then accelerated past her in formation, disappearing smoothly into the night.

She had already decided on her plan even before the encounter: she was going to leave the city. Disaster had been averted for now. She was going to find out what came next.

She was cycling into the future.

3: Dreams of the night highways and the dead suburbs

The dark hour before dawn. Which is when the human metabolism is at its nadir. Body temperature lowest, adrenalin zero, ushering in death.

In the depth of the undergrowth, something stirs. It's a suburban vixen, pausing in mid-prowl before an unfamiliar, and possibly dangerous smell. Her ears prick. Not for the first time, she has penetrated the half-abandoned garden a few hundred yards from her lair, where two hours ago she left her hungry cubs waiting underground, mewing and fidgeting. Now she's located the strange odour: it comes from an inchoate bundle in the bushes, part covered with leaves.

In the road below, the attack phase of a car engine's hum is accompanied by a quick flash of headlights; then the sound decays over several seconds back into silence.

Not quite silence. Other animals prowl in the night. The fieldmouse skitters nervously, sensing the vixen, finding the broken entrance to the old bird-house which long ago fell off its perch into the long grass. The young frog, graduated this summer from the garden pond, hops then freezes. The barn owl utters his solemn imprecation before gliding down from a branch to swoop low over the undergrowth and its sleeping form. In a neighbouring field, a mare pony moves to nudge her foal, uttering a low snort. Collectively, it is as though the night creatures watch over the human bundle, the sleeping child, whose eyelashes tremble, a drop of dew on them, the black earth wanting to swallow her up. It's as though their loving gaze makes a sanctuary, a margin of safety till night has almost passed away.

Here, the city's pall holds no sway, and the high scudding

clouds have left a gap through which the glorious night sky, including the setting moon, has shone unseen for hours on the sleeping child.

The vixen's still cautious. The bundle clearly poses no threat, but already the eastern sky is lightening imperceptibly, and the delicate balance of the animal's senses is disturbed. Making a discreet circle around the bundle, she deftly sneaks away towards the perimeter fence, patterning the soft ground with her black feet. She cuts a diagonal path across the over-grown garden, pausing before she ventures onto the exposed lawn, bearing past the skirt of the old shed. Perhaps it once held chickens. Not now.

Is that a failing satellite among the myriad stars? Is the earth rushing towards it?

The scent of earth is powerful.

The night's bundle stirs and wakes. Her thoughts are inco-herent; there are leaves at her lips, air chill ices her blood. Maybe she caught the vixen's sharp smell. The barn owl, his watching done for the night, flaps noiselessly away to the aban-doned railway buildings where he has made his home. The fieldmouse leaves the sanctuary of the broken bird-house and makes straight for the damp entrance to her home in the bank. The frog lies buried under moss. The dark mare and her foal stand almost still in the shelter of the hedge, faint steam rising from their backs. What was that sudden brisk movement across the sky, its suddenness becoming an interrupted continuity or a repeated discontinuity? A tiny black flitting thing: probably a bat, on its last nocturnal excursion before settling into the loft of the old house.

She is only half awake yet. The illusion is broken. The circle of animal magic that appeared to protect her for the past few hours begins to disperse. The animals, after all, were only going about their night's business, neither benevolently nor malevo-lently disposed towards her, but simply accepting her as a new element of the complex ecology in which they participated every night.

Straight above her, where there'd recently been total blackness are now outlined (against an almost purple sky) the black branching shapes of trees beginning to lose their leaves to the advancing autumn. (It has advanced considerably further here than in the centre of the metropolis.) The world starts to reveal itself once again, slowly and without discernible purpose.

Her leg is cold. No, upgrade that, it's frozen. The coat she's pulled over herself has drifted in the night, taking with it part of the impromptu heap of dead leaves she gathered. The skin of her cheek has been bitten by the hardness of her shoulder bag used as a pillow. Her hair feels tangled, her eyelids gummed. She is stiff and miserable. She sits up.

Dawn. In the distance, the rumble of a freight train, on its way to the coast. It slowly dies away. Its sound is the sound of loneliness departing.

Now she can see beside her on the ground, half-hidden among woody matter, the dull gleam of her bicycle, which has achieved horizontal status. There are dreams to remember. Withdrawing a hand from what warmth there is, she unzips a flap of her shoulder-bag and takes from it her new Chinese notebook, still pristine, and a stubby pencil.

•

But it was hard to separate dreams from reality. There'd been city streets, brightly lit at first, then darkening as she left the centre and cycled further into the night; and then mile upon mile of wide highways, whereon she'd had to suffer repeatedly the buffeting wind of a massive articulated lorry overtaking her on its own course out of the city and towards the distant sea-ports. And the headlights of the vehicles opposite, coming at her undipped. Then for hours the highway had been flooded with yellow from the tall sodium lamps that punctuated it, until finally these too had given out and there was only starlight and the occasional gleam from a distant industrial estate. Few lights glowed in the ribbon development of housing that followed the road; everybody in these suburbs had gone to bed by now. And the only other illumination was the feeble glow of her own headlamp on the patch of road ahead, giving movement an illusion of solidity, however vulnerable.

The city at this hour, seen from above, from a landmapping satellite perhaps, would have resembled a dying galaxy. Lights one by one winking off, though leaving a residual brilliance at the centre. The generated glow would never completely subside. (Astronomers called it "light pollution"; it made scanning of the heavens impossible, and for this reason the national observatory had years ago moved out from its ancient base by the metropolitan river, into the hinterland.) The landmapping satellite would have observed a tracery of street lighting marking the roads leading out of the city; moving lights along these pathways showed the motion of the articulated trucks and other intermittent night traffic; but you would have had to zoom in much closer to detect the glow of Eye's lamp as it inched along one of the intersecting southern routes, and closer still to discern her pedalling form, wrapped in her new coat, her head clad in its silk scarf, her wool-covered legs pumping rhythmically, her uncovered cold hands whitely grasping the handlebars.

Illuminated signs loomed up, and disappeared behind her. Sometimes she stopped at an intersection to let sparse traffic go by, but, this aside, her pace was steady, as though she knew where she was heading.

At a certain junction, finally, she turned off to the left, entering first an avenue of tall black trees, probably cypresses, and later, via a deserted roundabout presided over by the dim and monstrous shape of a war memorial, the beginnings of a suburban high street. There was no traffic here at all; the big lorries all used the by-pass.

At the mouth of the high street, suddenly, a snow-blinding light and the smell of oil. An all-night petrol station. She steered into its concourse, past the pumps, and came to rest by a pair of glass doors, against which she propped the bike.

A boy sat in the office. He was reading a paperback science fiction novel; on its cover (she could see) a huge dying sun loomed behind a ruined 20th century city, its three remaining denizens in the foreground, hands on hips, wearing dark glasses. To the boy's right were the retail shelves: sugar in its various guises, repair kits, "gifts". Potted plants in cellophane, pre-recorded cassettes at bargain prices, motor oil (a free jug and beaker with each can), cigarettes, telephones, coloured plastic storage boxes stacked to the ceiling. But although the boy himself was bathed in fluorescence the lights on the products were dimmed to indicate the section was closed.

The boy did not seem surprised to see her. Sweetness emanated slowly from him. His eyes were ringed darkly, as though made up; he wore jeans and a sweatshirt silkscreened with the name of a rock band (the name slightly cracked on the cotton fabric). He put down his book when she came in and smiled.

So did she.

"What're you reading?" asked Eye, pulling the silk scarf back off her head.

He handed her the book. She studied the blurb.

"A portrait of a city which has suffered a disaster so cataclysmic that the very fabric of the space-time continuum has been distorted.... Buildings burn endlessly but are not consumed. Radio and television broadcasts cannot enter or leave the city. The sky is sealed with thick haze. When it clears, strange portents are seen...."

"That's right."

"Sounds good." She handed it back to him.

Was he an angel? His dark hair, she noticed, was gathered into a short ponytail. It was gathered rather high on the head, and only the hair from a small area had been scraped together, leaving a pale circle of scalp surrounding the root of the tail, a feature which could have served as a halo. She decided if he was an angel he was a benevolent one.

Although almost certain where she was, she asked him for directions. The name of the suburban town which was her objective — nowadays almost enveloped within the sprawl of the greater city, but theoretically retaining its historical integrity still — was confirmed.

"You're right on the edge of it."

Then they both laughed; that was a joke, because the name of the band on his sweatshirt also incorporated the notion of "edge".

"Where are you going?" he politely asked.

And she replied: "I'm cycling into the future." She said it in a way which maintained the good humour. How far are you going, was the boy's next question. To which Eye answered, "As far as it takes me." He laughed again then, which pleased her.

The boy: I've been travelling too.

Eye: So you don't live here, then?

The boy: It's OK for a while, but it's a bit of a suburban dump.

He meant the district they were in. She couldn't quite place his accent, vestigial as it was, but it was flavoured with bigger spaces than were achievable here, in the environs of the city. It spoke of a more languorous life among extensive jagged coast-lines and rolling foothills. She asked him then where he came from, and he told her. A house laced with ironwork near a beach where ocean breakers rolled in; wide avenues bordered with evergreen trees; big, unkempt cars; strange animals that lived in the hills; the proximity of painters, sculptors, mechanics, beachcombers, alcoholics; a brilliant sun that never faded from view for long, never succumbed to the dying fall of the end of the year; loud radio in the streets; vast quantities of fruit just rotting if you didn't eat them; the always distant hum of the expressway; breezes ruffling the harbour water; the heat driving through from the hinterland.

But he'd grown restless and bored after a while, he said, had decided to take a trip with some friends in an old truck, heading for that hinterland, in the direction of the blue distant mountains that was where his future lay, at least he'd thought so for a while, the ropy truck stacked with beer, they'd shoot the animals of the desert for their food and roast the haunches on an open fire; only it turned out to be a disaster, one of them contracted dysentery, two others had fallen out with each other, the truck broke down on the dusty red road inconveniently equidistant from two settlements, and we were talking long distance here; the one with dysentery almost died, it took him (the boy) half a day's walking to fetch help in the shape of water and a telephone, they got him to hospital at last, the two others not speaking, and that was the end of that adventure.

Unsatisfied, the boy'd invested most of his remaining savings in a plane ticket that took him across the world; he'd heard that the natives of a certain mountain community played this incredible music dating from what journalists liked to call the dawn of time, so he wanted to hear this; and he spent weeks in an ancient white city whose crumbling stone towers and minarets were interspersed with jungles of TV aerials and satellite dishes, and at last found someone in a gloomy cafe where the men all had hot drinks in glasses and played chess and backgammon, the friend of a friend of a student at the American college, who told him where the music could be found, but it would cost him; he'd had no money when he arrived but he'd made some with a piece of work the student had put his way, a bit of translation, also by selling his watch, though he was determined to keep the personal cassette recorder which he could have got quite a bit for, also by reselling to other students a proportion of a certain illicit substance he'd acquired on arrival; he had few living expenses because he slept in a little tent on the beach which he rolled up every morning and carried around with him everywhere, and food was cheap in the market, though you had to be careful and wash all the fruit in mineral water. And at last he was taken to the mountain community and met the men who played the music; they smoked all the time and wore white robes over tee-shirts advertising well-known soft drinks, and they slammed their drums and blew their pipes into a frenzy, it was in celebration of a local wedding, the bride just a little girl really, smiling shyly, averting her eyes; he got it all down on cassette, they were extremely kind to him, fed him, gave him beer which they really weren't supposed to drink themselves but they did.

Then when he had taken his leave he went back to the city, caught the ferry; spent all morning trying to dodge a middle-aged white man in a cream suit who pursued him all over the boat; whichever deck he chose to escape to there the man already was, he couldn't tell whether this was a police agent in search of that same substance or whether he was simply after the boy's body; became paranoid; took the rolled-up tent, which he still carried, into one of the ferry's toilets with him and unrolled it, pretty difficult in that confined space, especially with people shuffling outside and sometimes trying the door, paranoid that one of them might be the man in the cream suit, retrieving the piece of substance that nestled deep within the innermost fold of the tent, refolded it, it was impossible, made a fist of it anyway, and re-emerged to a funny look from another fellow-passenger, made his way to the top deck, oh god there the guy was again, finally made it, threw the small foil-wrapped brick sorrowfully into the dancing wake, among the occasional flash of a dolphin following the vessel.

Ironically, he then never saw the man in the cream suit again, it was as though he too had jumped off into the sea. On disembarking, he hitched his way along shimmering roads, up into more mountains, skirting industrial cities polluted with the fumes from oil refineries, stopping off once or twice to wander through a vast mediaeval cathedral, his dwarfed face washed with stained glass light, a crick in his neck from gazing in the gloom, getting lost among a forest of variegated pillars that echoed and loomed, being silently admonished by pious marble; then onward, via another ferry, eventually arriving with nothing but an address hastily scribbled on a scrap of paper at the outskirts of the city where Eye lived, these very outskirts in fact where they now were in the small hours of the night, where the future, he said, had momentarily been suspended due to another cash shortage.

All of this Eye heard, perched on a counter in front of the boy, her legs dangling lazily, her eyes fixed on his, nodding every now and then. But the future, she objected, the future is always there, everybody's facing it, you can't stop it, in fact it's already there. What does that mean, he said. It means you just have to open your eyes, she said, you can go further into the future than ever before if you really want, just open your eyes and pedal! You could, he said, you could reach the future before anyone else, if you had a bicycle that was capable of colossal speed, that could approach the speed of light. That would be a great idea, he said, getting carried away again by his own rhetoric, a bike that could approach the speed of light. As you approached the speed of light you became compressed in the direction of travel, that was according to Einstein, your personal space became constricted, that is, compared to everything else, but you wouldn't notice it yourself of course, nor would you notice that your wristwatch if you wore one (Eye didn't, she said) was going slower and slower, in other words your personal time was slowing down, again compared to everything else, though to you it would be as though time in the rest of the universe was speeding up, at first looking like one of those old silent films that are projected at the wrong speed nowadays so everyone walks round in incredibly jerky flashes, then speeding up even from that so everything just becomes a blur, and when at last you slow down, come back to your starting point, come to rest, you're home, only you're not home at all. Because, although you think you've only been gone a few hours or a few days, years have passed in the world that you knew, centuries, everyone that you knew and cared for has long since died, your own great-great-grandchildren whom you've never seen are older than you, there's nobody else, it's a completely new and alien world. It shines with newness but it's lonely, because you're the only person from the past in it. You've found the future, and it's beautiful but lonely.

Yes, but let's suppose, wondered Eye, what if, let's forget reaching the speed of light, but what if the bicycle only took you up to a fraction of the speed of light, just a tiny minute fraction, wouldn't that give you a little push? Just a little push into the future? Perhaps you would be a split second into the future, rather than centuries, but that would be OK, that's all you'd want. Just a split second, well it would be unnoticeable, everything would be just the same, almost. Not quite. You would sense it. You would sense that things were not quite the same. It would be like the present except there'd be a freshness about everything, it would all be newly born.

The boy considered. "Wouldn't that be something?" he agreed.

Eye: I think it's possible, because I can feel it.

She looked at her small, bangled hand on the counter: was it compressed at all? Had her personal dimensions, the physical space she occupied, been fractionally diminished and her time correspondingly extended? But whatever, it was late. It was late in whichever world she inhabited now. "I have to go on," she said, jumping down to the floor.

The boy: Nice talking to you. It gets boring here all night.

Eye said: "I hope you make it, into your future." Then, indicating the displayed product range from which fluorescence had been withdrawn: "I haven't eaten for a while; isn't the shop open?"

He shook his head; the ponytail swayed. "But hang on a second." Leaping up, he disappeared behind a shelf. Seconds later, he reappeared with two chocolate bars, which he handed her.

When she made as though to look for money, he waved her aside. "Take care." It was the first unsolicited kindness she had had since her office colleague had escorted her to the bathroom when she'd collapsed at the computer screen. When had that been? Less than 24 hours ago. Their time, anyway.

"And you."

The boy returned to his book.

Then there was darkness once more. The high street was full of ghosts. Shuttered banks and a post office, a hotel with a glow in one window, darkened displays of shoes behind glass, one shop window dimly and greenishly illuminated to reveal exotic plants, and perhaps products for their care. The street itself was as if freshly laundered, shining under its lamps from time to time. Her tyres made a fresh continuous sizzle in the middle of it, which almost echoed from both sides. Beside this dead commerce the whole sky looked monumental. She heard the chime of a distant church clock. One, two, three. As forlorn as the sound of a blackbird trapped in a chimney.

Darkness, and silence. The smell of vegetation. An unmade side road, and then a gate. It creaked.

The house ahead was quite still. Nobody would be up at this hour.

Carefully, she wheeled the bike through the gate, which swung slowly to behind her, and halfway up the path. She was very tired.

On her left was a shed. But it was padlocked shut.

Her legs suddenly wanted her to sink.

She wheeled the bike into the undergrowth and laid it there on its side. She sat down among some dry, comforting leaves. Fortunately, it had not rained for some time. She ate the two chocolate bars the boy in the petrol station had given her. Then she lay down. With great slow swings of her arms she swept as many of the leaves as she could over her. Just for a few minutes. But it was here that the animals of the night later found her asleep.

•

The memory of a dream began to struggle into consciousness. She was in the satellite, which was moving over the earth. The interior of the satellite was a labyrinth of endless galleries. But no, not quite endless: an end was within reach; she could sense it. Confused sounds, whispers, rumours assailed her. The passage spiralled inward to the heart of the mystery. And there, up ahead, was the doorway into it. She touched the steel door.

It slid noiselessly open. She stepped through.

Immediately, the sounds stopped. She was looking down on a great hushed auditorium, row on row of empty seats raking down in an almost complete circle around a spotlit emptiness. Warm glows bathed the only two figures in that sea; when they turned round together, she saw they were Dee and Zoo. They smiled at her, and waved her down, as though inviting her to witness the explanation, which would shortly arrive on the spotlit platform. They were radiant, and completely naked. Except that their entire bodies, even to the nipples on their breasts, were covered in a fine golden fur or down. They beckoned to her. And she noticed for the first time that she was naked too, and covered with the same fur.

The auditorium's rows of seats banked down towards the central stage, where something would emerge into the spotlight. Something frightful....

That was what had awoken her. She put the Chinese notebook and pencil back into her bag, and stiffly stood up. Darkness, and silence. The smell of the garden in her nostrils. But not quite darkness now, definitely a lack of totality to it, the sky purpling into dawn.

What did it reveal? The shape of a house. Massive, anyway. And that sound was no longer a church bell. A blackbird, trying voice.

She draped anew the coat round her shoulders, shuddering, and drew one leg and then the other up, rubbing the calves vigorously through the cloth of her trousers. Ice blue on the grass ahead.

It was a chunky stone farmhouse that appeared from amid its unkempt garden. She was viewing it at an angle of 45 degrees, the front facing to her left, the side losing itself to her right in shadow and trees. It was squat: two storeys, gabled roof tiled not slated. The ground floor windows now distinctly leaded. The upper windows half hidden under the dark downward thrust of the gable. At the front, a porch; and here, three solid pillars supporting the roof overhang.

Beside it, to the left, was a shed or perhaps a garage, its doors padlocked.

Birds were beginning to twitter more profusely now, and once she heard a car door slam somewhere and the engine start up, coughing once or twice before its roar. She leaned down to touch her bicycle; it was slightly damp with a skin of dew. As she was doing this, a blackbird dropped to the uneven stretch of lawn in front of her (between her and the house), hopped about for a bit and then, perhaps noticing her, flew abruptly off.

She stretched. Head tipped slightly to one side, she tested the emanations from the house. She could detect nothing.

Cautiously, she began to find a way through the tangled undergrowth. There was some sort of a path hacked through which nevertheless she had to mend from time to time by pulling away thorny branches. Once a spider's web delicately brushed her face. In this fashion she skirted the house until after a while she was facing its back, where the undergrowth was slightly less dense; in fact, there was a patch where it had been completely cleared and the almost bare (weedy) earth was punctuated by what looked like thick cabbage plants gone to seed. Further off was a vertical wooden pole which had evidently once supported a bird house; it lay in pieces in the bushes where it had fallen. A stone path wandered off aimlessly in search of more trees to lose itself in. Aware deep within her of a possibility of danger, she followed this, then branched off it into a climb which led her to a higher level. Here, there was another shed, made of brick, with a broken roof. Blackness gaped where a door should have been. She peered inside: dank nothingness, a gap beyond and a broken rail. Fear began to well. Quickly she turned away.

There was something both familiar and unfamiliar about the garden. And also something both comforting and menacing. But it was her only chance. That's what she said to herself. What did she mean when she thought that?

By now the sky had turned several shades of blue, from indigo in the west to pale cyan in the east. She could hear the road's incipient traffic growing to a low-key roar punctuated by silences. On the far side was the thickety boundary to the garden. Instead of going that far, she descended via another path which she hit by accident, as weed-grown as everything else. At one point it went under a broken rustic arch. Skirting a small pond, it returned her smartly to the front lawn. Across it, she saw the gleam of the bicycle in the bushes where she'd slept.

There had been a change. Now there was a light in an upper window at the front of the house. Her heart began to beat faster. But surely there was nothing bad in the house?

Eye crossed the lawn now, her feet crunching, and retrieved her bag and bike, returning the latter to its upright position.

Then, hooking the bag over her shoulder, she wheeled the bike up to the porch. As she was doing this, she heard the gate clang shut behind her.

A man with a sack approached the porch too, holding a bundle of letters in his hand.

"Good morning," the postman greeted her.

Immediately, she replied, "Thanks, I'll take those."

He handed the bundle over, quickly turned back towards the gate, opened and carefully shut it behind him as he started off up the lane to resume his round.

The door, blue and solid, incorporated a heavy black knocker. Now or never. But what would she say when her knock was answered? She lifted the knocker once, twice, letting it rap smartly each time.

After a while, there was a faint noise within the house. All at once something flapped at her calves. A small black cat emerged from its cat-door and looked up at her suspiciously. It sidled past, making for the lawn.

Seconds later, the door itself opened. A tall, youngish man stood there. He had dishevelled hair, an olive pullover, jeans and brown slippers.

His eyebrows, knitted till that moment, shot up; his mouth opened, but not much.

Eye smiled shyly. Another fragment of memory returned, floating to the surface like detritus from a wreck.

Without a word, she handed him the letters. I think these are yours, the gesture said.

He said, aloud: "Jesus Christ."

Eye: No, John, it's me!

He: Eileen!

Eye: Oh, is it OK to leave my bike in your porch?

He (distractedly): Yes ... oh heavens, you better come in.

•

"You mean you spent the night in the garden?" he demanded incredulously, pouring hot coffee from a glass jug into her mug.

It was cosy in this kitchen beside the boiler, even though the floor was bare boards and there were no curtains at the window.

Eye, cradling the mug, admitted: "Only a couple of hours really. I arrived after three in the morning. It was all dark. I was trying to figure out how to get into the house without disturbing anyone. Then I thought I might sleep in the garage, but it was padlocked. By the time I thought all this out, well, I kind of fell asleep."

"You'll be lucky if you don't catch pneumonia!" he scolded.

So solicitous about her welfare, and so endearingly patronising. This was what he had always been like, she thought. He spoke to her as though he knew her well, as though he had the right to.

John went on:

"You'll never cease being strange, will you? You always did everything back to front, and inside out. Anybody else would just come and visit me. You know, like normal people. You catch the 9.35 train one Saturday morning, arrive here, we go for a walk, we have lunch, maybe we go and see a film at the local, then you stay over, or OK, maybe you go back in the evening. But that doesn't appeal, does it? No, you have to arrive in the middle of the night, without phoning first ..."

"I did try, there was no answer ..."

"... without checking first, we could've been away. But then, I suppose I don't remember when you last phoned. I'd given up trying. Do you know, I was thinking about you only yesterday, I don't know why, it was while I was in the supermarket in town with Nancy, and I suddenly had this kind of premonition, you know that awful cold certainty, that I would never see you again. After last week. I was thinking, right, that's a closed chapter. And here you are ..." (he shook his head, wryly smiling) "... out of the blue, a frozen stick on your bicycle, talking about the future.... You're lucky you didn't get reported to the cops by the neighbours, they think we're disreputable enough. Do you want some toast?"

Of course, she was thinking, it's Saturday. Yesterday was a Friday. She had not burned her boats yet. At work they would have assumed she'd taken the rest of the day off because of the accident with the computer.

What she said was: "After last week. You said after last week. What do you mean?"

He stared at her. "I mean after the party."

She had to stop herself, at the last possible instant, saying, what party. Instead, measuring her words out carefully, "Well, that's not so odd then, that you thought of me. If you'd seen me a week before."

He said: "Not so odd? I don't know. You turned up, I didn't really expect you to reply to the invitation, given the length of time, the years since … well, you know. Then I hardly saw you all evening, and you disappeared without a word. A week later I'm thinking about you, and the next day suddenly here you are again, out of the blue."

The door was kicked open. It banged, and bounced back, then opened again more gently.

A little girl of about five entered the room. She was wearing a nightdress with frills down the front, and her feet were bare. Her fair hair was long and rumpled. She looked sleepy and sulky. She gave no sign of recognising Eye, and offered no greeting.

John scolded again: "I told you not to kick the door like that. Come in and meet Eileen. This is Nancy. Nancy, I don't think you remember Eileen. You were only a tiny baby when you last saw her."

The child merely scowled, and rubbed her left eye with her right hand, contorting her arm over her head to do it, so that the small fist pointed downward as it rubbed.

Eye: Hello, Nancy. Didn't I … meet you at the party?

John (glancing at Eye oddly): No, of course you didn't. She was in bed. Were you that … er, inebriated?

Nancy: What's inebulated?

John: Never mind.

Nancy: I want cornflakes.

John: In a minute, darling.

Nancy (to Eye): Have you come to stay?

Eye: I'm not sure how long I'll be staying.

Nancy: Daddy said we could go for a walk in Cuckoo Wood today. The other people who live here, who are the owners of this house, are away. They went to the seaside. Daddy says we've been to the seaside several times this summer so we can't go. Would you like to come for a walk?

Eye: I'd like that very much.

Nancy: We'll see the ponies in the field. They belong to the gypsies. Sometimes the gypsies come and do their washing in the laundrette. And do you know, they have so much washing they use up every single drier at the same time!

She had dropped her sulky look, and her eyes shone with excitement now as she spoke about the laundrette and the gypsies.

John brought toast to the table, and scrambled eggs, and poured milk over Nancy's cornflakes. He refilled the coffee mugs. The big boiler shuddered into life. Sunshine began to trickle through the smudged glass of the window. At last, if only for a brief time, Eye felt at peace.

•

She inhabited a privileged zone, a world of appearances that accommodated itself so readily to her needs that it was a shock whenever she was forced to realise that she was faking it. Her presence, that is, so impalpable because what was underpinning it was so fragile.

What was that Zoo had said yesterday morning, which had sent her into such an inexplicable spin? "Ghosts. There may be four of us in this house, you know." Perhaps it was she, after all, who was the ghost. Yet at this minute it didn't seem to worry her. It was easy being a ghost.

The little girl, Nancy, for instance, had accepted her so readily, so touchingly. There she was, running eagerly away up the overgrown path, in her jeans and sweater, while she and John followed behind. Now she even recalled a tiny, squalling baby in the space where the girl was. Yes, that would have been perhaps five years ago, or a little less.

Where did the gap begin then? Because there was a gap. What, for instance, had happened last week?

The way John spoke to her: easily, with a proprietorial hint, yet also warily at times. As though he was afraid of making the wrong move. So that gave her some power.

A sudden thought stopped her dead. Nancy's mother.... where was she, then? And this garden? Somewhere there had been a garden. Was it this one? A blackbird. Bye bye. Half-demolished brick, insects, the smell of damp. The soft sounds of conversation in the distance. Someone (who?) touched her face, and immediately she couldn't breathe, the world that had both scared and exhilarated her with its space now began to close in. The air thick, and trying to pant great gulps of it. She tried to tell herself she had never been in this garden before, just to see if that worked.

John was going, "Here's my latest effort at growing our own veg, as you can see, not any more successful than before. I think I'm going to give up. The soil's too chalky —" He broke off when he saw her stopped still about two yards behind him. "Eileen? What's the matter? Are you OK?"

Giving him a wintry smile, she came up beside him. "Yes, I'm fine."

He touched her arm then, the first touch there had been, and she didn't flinch but she didn't respond either. "I guess it can't ever be the same again," he said gently.

"No."

He showed her the rest of the overgrown garden. And it began to be familiar again now, with the strange familiarity of a dream half-recalled. But what she couldn't figure out was the extent to which this was a function of survival technique, a rapid mapping of unfamiliar surroundings. It reminds me of ... another garden, she said, a garden I saw in my dream. Through a window. But I might have been dreaming of this garden, you never know — and he looked at her strangely again then. You're obviously not sure whether you've been here before, he said, and when she glanced at him, startled, she realised he meant this as a joke. Of course, she agreed quickly, entering into the spirit of the jest, it's my rotten memory. There again was the stark pole and she could picture the bird-house, its scattered fragments joined once more, perching on top of it. Clematis and honeysuckle clung to the back wall of the house, and she could imagine their first buds, smell their first scent; logs lay half-chopped in an arbour as though she herself had only just put down the axe. The small frog pond was dark and bereft of life, yet she could see instantly the frantic spring scene of amphibian copulation. The little black cat curled up asleep in a patch of morning sun-light, why, she could remember it as a kitten, playing with a silver ribbon. All these memories, and she couldn't distinguish between the real ones and the false ones any more. But she had only to choose her words carefully, and all would be well, he would not suspect, what might he suspect, that she wasn't who she said she was. But she hadn't said she was anyone. All she'd said was she was cycling into the future; the rest he had supplied.

Let's have lunch, he was saying now, and then we'll go for a walk to Cuckoo Wood.

They were approaching the second, ruined shed, behind the house. There was something wrong about it. She didn't like it.

Nancy had been hiding in it; she jumped out at them, laughing, and they both pretended to be frightened.

•

"You're an innocent," he told her. "That's because I forget everything," Eye said, sweetly. At this, he smiled.

It was an intermittently sunny afternoon, but with clouds scudding across the sky, and a brisk breeze attempting semi-violent caresses. Eye had got her blue scarf wrapped round her face. John was in a blue anorak and black bobble hat. Nancy, after much grumbling, had been persuaded to wear a red coat with integral hood.

They crossed the main road, went through a gate, and started to climb a winding lane which led past a modern hous-ing estate and thence away from the build-up of suburbia towards Cuckoo Wood.

"What do you mean," said John, "cycling into the future?"

Eye considered. "I want to discover it. I want to discover the future. I have to."

John: Do you, does one, discover the future or invent it? I don't know, it seems to me more like something you invent. Like, where was gravity before Newton discovered it?

Eye: OK, invent if you like. Invent is better. Though I don't know about gravity. Didn't things fall down before, or wasn't that "gravity" then, in inverted commas?

John: Anyway, we're all travelling into the future. That's the only way we can go.

Eye: Yeah, but maybe we're travelling at different rates. Maybe some of us get there before others.

John: Get there? The whole point is, you never get there.

Eye: Yes, I think you do.

John: So how do you know when you've got there? How do you know when you've arrived at the future? And what happens to the past and the present then?

Eye: The past isn't real. I … feel I … haven't got a past any more. How do I know when I arrive? It'll feel, oh, different. I'll know. And the present will be my past again.

John (shaking his head indulgently): You've lost me there!

Eye: The future is where everything is transformed.

John: That's a very romantic view. Did you ever read The Time Machine? I read it when I was a kid, it made a big impression on me. You know, when the Time Traveller arrives in the future in his ivory and brass machine — it sounds a bit like your bicycle — he says something like "I flung myself into futurity" — when he arrives, he finds a paradise. He's on a lawn, in a warm and sunny garden, with wonderful fruit and flowers, where eight hundred thousand years ago there was a city, and gentle people, hippies really, a serene life of indolence…. So I suppose I know what you mean in a way. But then what happens? What happens when night comes? The dark side….

Eye (interrupting): I know all that. But it's not a garden of Eden I want. It's a transformation of now. That's what the future is. Even in the city.

John: Ah, the city. Look, we can see the city now.

So they could. They had left behind them the ugly square council housing blocks, and had reached a crest, a paved area in front of chain-link fencing that held back the woodland. Below and to the north lay the city from which Eye had cycled, a pall laid patchily upon it, yet distant tower-block windows gleaming the reflection of a momentarily hidden sun. The sprawl lapped around the occasional island of green, its metal and concrete components massively duned, punctuated in one or two places by a tall communications tower guyed by semi-invisible silver ropes. They stopped to look, while Nancy skipped on ahead, humming.

John: You see — the future is a very old-fashioned notion, isn't it? It's — oh, I don't know — multicoloured biplanes zooming through skyscraper canyons, and all the buildings are like the Chrysler building in New York. That's Progress with a capital P. Does anybody believe that any more?

Eye: Hmmm.

John: Do you?

Eye: That stuff, about biplanes and skyscrapers. That's only because those science fiction writers were writing years ago. And they were really only describing their present. But that's all it is, that's what I'm saying. Perhaps it's the present, what's the word, transfigured. What transfigures it, is what you can't describe, because you can't know it.

John: So the future is the unknown? You want to know the unknown?

Eye: Yes.

John: The future is the unknown; which is the sacred, the divine. You want a transfiguration of the present, really, you're talking about the invention of the unknown as a way of sanctifying the present. I remember feeling like that when I was a kid, though I couldn't put it into those words at the time. I even remember vividly one instant, when I was walking to school, and thinking, I really wanted to trap the next moment. Futile wish. I think I was conscious for almost the first time that, although this was the present moment, as soon as I'd even

91

had that thought it would no longer be so, it would be the past. Perhaps I was an odd child. And I said to myself, it was as I was climbing some ruined steps beside a church, on my way to school, I said to myself, I wonder whether, if I concentrate enough, I'll remember this moment when nothing happened except that I had this thought. Well, as you now know, because I'm telling you, I did, and do. We are now in that moment's future, if you like. But as for the future in general, well, there's no future for that — everything is known, in terrifying detail, everything has been invented now, hasn't it? In a sense, there's no future left any more.

Eye: That's not true. How can everything have been invented? I won't believe that.

John: You sound like the adherent of some obsolete religion. It's always sunny and wonderful in your future. Your optimism is touching, but it doesn't convince me. Imagine what this place, that place (indicating the city) would be like in eight hundred thousand years, or even just eight hundred years, if we just did nothing but dream about it. I mean, look at the city. It certainly could do with some transfiguration. Look at all those industries. Factories, refineries, plants of all kinds, pumping out their pollutants into the atmosphere. Burning up the rapidly diminishing fossil fuels and pumping out shit into the atmosphere, sulphuric acid which falls on us in the rain, carbon dioxide which builds up and will pretty soon begin to cause catastrophic warming of the planet. Already you can see what the future holds, in more and more freakish weather conditions. Like this so-called Indian summer we've been having, very nice isn't it, but not so good when the world's agricultures go to pot, deserts creep onward, rising sea levels cause flooding in coastal areas. That's what our civilisation, our industry is doing to the future! Not to mention the traffic, clogging up the roads. You should see the by-pass on a weekday: nose-to-tail cars exhaling their fumes, and most of them with only one person inside! Then when they've all somehow got to work, it's the turn of the big juggernauts coming up from the coast, belching out lead fallout at God knows what rate. I tell you, it's not even worth my growing vegetables anyway in that garden of ours, I read somewhere they'd be steeped in lead, most of them, especially the ones that grow above ground. I don't want my daughter's brain-cells atrophied! And the waste! Can you imagine the amount of garbage produced in just one suburb like this? On the other side of the wood, I'll show you, there's a dump, a bank behind a row of houses right where the railway goes, where people have just offloaded anything they don't want: old refrigerators just rolled down the slope, rusting away, plastic packaging, old tyres, cardboard boxes, plastic oil-drums. Just dumped in what used to be a woodland clearing. And aerosol cans thrown away, as if they haven't already done enough damage by releasing chlorofluorocarbons into the stratosphere, puncturing the ozone layer and letting in all sorts of harmful radiation from the sun. And it isn't just industry and cities — not far from here agribusiness is destroying the natural countryside, bulldozing hedgerows and other natural habitats for wild creatures, woodlands that have existed for thousands of years, all gone, and they're polluting the earth and poisoning us with pesticides and nitrates, ruining the environment forever just for short-term profit. Once all this was woodland. Then there was a small farming town here. Our farmhouse dates from then. Now it's just a suburb of the big city, everything's been swallowed up by shopping precincts, industry and factory agriculture. You talk about the future? Forget it. The future is heat death. Everywhere will be the same as everywhere else, dreary, sterile, scorched. Oh yes, and then there's the destruction of the rain-forests, I tell you what that does....

Eye: Have you always been this miserable?

John: You should know me by now.

Eye: I should?

•

It was cool in Cuckoo Wood, but pleasantly sheltered from the stiff breeze on the ridge. Birds chattered in the beech trees above them. A liquid warble was answered from another direction by staccato chirps. Now a trill, now the cawing of an inland seagull flying unseen overhead, above the half-denuded canopy of the trees. Ferns brushed their faces, gorse and thorns on the brambles prickled them as they passed. Their shoes on the path made the quantities of fallen leaves speak. In one stretch, the path had been marked for walkers by thin slices of log laid serially, and there were clearings designated as picnic spots; in other places nature had scorned such manicuring. At one point, in a clearing, they had to clamber round the trunk of a great elm, uprooted in recent storms; at another, they skirted segregated conifers.

Nancy jogged happily, brandishing a gnarled long twig or short branch she had picked up from among the fallen leaves. "Look at me, I'm a shepherd!" she screamed in delight. She had wriggled her arms out of the sleeves of her coat, while keeping the hood on, so that it flapped around her like a red cape. "You look more like Little Red Riding Hood," observed Eye, wondering even as she spoke how naturally such a remark came. "Shall I be the big bad wolf?" suggested John, pretending to snarl and curling the fingers of each hand to resemble claws. At this, Nancy squealed in delight and ran away at top speed, still clutching her branch.

John said, suddenly: "I'm in love."

Eye (mildly startled): Who with?

John: I don't know — I haven't met her yet. I mean, have you ever met anybody to whom you could say: "I love you so much I want to share my telephone bill with you"? I've done that. It didn't work.

Eye (smiling): No.

John: You know what I'm talking about. I've thought about you from time to time. And how it was — once. But I know it could never work out. It would be so attractive to go off and live in the country. I mean the real country, if it still exists. The farmhouse is nice, but as I said we've been swallowed up by suburbia. Sooner or later, they'll want to put a shopping mall in our road.

Eye (still smiling): I deeply hate the countryside, you know.

John: You don't really, but so you've often told me.

Eye: Have I? I'm sorry.

John: There's no need to be, Eileen. I know I'm a gloomy old bastard.

She looked at the stern set of his mouth; he'd removed his black woollen hat and now a hank of hair kept slipping over his chunky brow, and had to be pushed back again with a quick movement of the hand. "Knowledge is in that face," she thought, and knew obscurely she'd had that thought before. "But knowledge alone isn't everything."

There was a scream from Nancy. Where was she?

John ran into a thicket from which the sound had come, followed closely by Eye.

Nancy threw herself upon him, sobbing. She hadn't let go of the branch, and it got tangled in his hair. "What is it, darling?" But Eye had already seen the cause of the distress. On the ground, half-covered by leaves, was the dull brown-grey carcass of a fox.

It lay stiffly, its legs like sticks, the head held on the ground at an odd angle. It didn't look real. It hadn't yet begun to decompose.

Eye said: "Has it been shot?"

"Probably poisoned by pesticides in something it ate," said John, after a cursory inspection.

"Can we bury it?" wailed the small girl.

"We could cover it up with the leaves," suggested Eye.

"Oh yes, let's do that!"

The tears had gone, like the end of a brief summer rain-squall, ferocious while it lasted but leaving little trace.

All three knelt on the ground and shovelled more of the dead leaves over the animal, Eye and John using their hands while Nancy ineffectually wielded the branch.

Nancy (anxiously): Is it, is it, Daddy, is it the same one we saw last winter?

John: No, I don't think so, dear. That was a vixen. This is a dog fox.

Nancy: Oh, yes.

Eye: Where did you see the vixen?

Nancy (eyes shining): In our garden! I remember it was winter 'cause there was all snow, it was really thick. I looked out of my bedroom window, really really early in the morning, it was nearly still dark, and there she was.

Eye: What was she doing?

Nancy: Well, I don't remember. Oh yes, she was walking across the lawn. But the lawn was all white 'cause there'd been snow falling in the night. And she left footprints all across it. She was walking slowly, she didn't hear me 'cause I was quiet as a mouse. Daddy saw her too from downstairs, didn't you, Daddy? She went right across the lawn and disappeared behind the shed. That's when I was four.

They continued on their walk, eventually leaving the wood and emerging into evening light. They skirted a golf course. Far below, three men in brightly coloured sweaters were having a bantering argument on the green, involving much uproarious laughter, but they were too far away to catch any of the substance of this discourse. The sun had gone down behind the brow of the hill opposite. Pink began to tinge the sky above it. "Lovely," said Eye. "Atmospheric pollution," said John.

Rows of houses loomed up. And finally the motorway, its freight of evening traffic making a low hum in the air.

A point of light in the sky.

Look, said John, the evening star.

Eye said: "It isn't the satellite?"

John: What satellite?

Eye: The one they say is going to drop back to earth.

John: I shouldn't think so.

Eye: I had a dream about it, you know. I dreamed I sort of heard it come down. And then I was actually in the satellite. It was like a spaceship, dark, with a labyrinth of passages inside. And I got lost.... (She shivered.)

Nancy: I've got a spaceship, Eileen. I got it for my birthday.

John: That wouldn't have been possible. That landmapping satellite: why, it's only a little thing. The main bit would have been hardly more than the size of that bicycle of yours.

Eye thought for a moment. She giggled. "A lunar cycle, or something!"

John: Oh dear, I wish I hadn't said that. Now I won't be able to stop thinking about it as a bicycle racing round above the stratosphere.

Eye: It's a nice thought.

But John actually didn't think so.

John: The trouble is my mind is too literal, or perhaps too visual. I have to have a visual image for everything. I ought to have been a painter, instead of a writer, maybe. When I read the first words of Wittgenstein's *Tractatus*, "The world is all that is the case", when I read that, I always see in my mind's eye a battered old suitcase.

Eye (excitedly): Why, I can see that suitcase too. But it's locked!

Nancy (whining insistently): What suitcase? What suitcase, Daddy?

John (sternly): It's all that is the case, not all that is in the case. For heaven's sake!

They crossed the motorway by the underpass, and a little later emerged onto a common by a row of shops. A wine shop's window glowed brightly now in the thickening evening. Eye went in to buy a bottle of wine, while John and Nancy remained outside, waiting for her. She had to delve into the front of her trousers while nobody was looking, to fish out a banknote with which to pay.

When she came out, Nancy was hopping up and down.

John: What is it, darling?

Nancy: The ponies! Pony, pony, pony!

John: Oh, yes, I forgot. Let's go and see them.

They made a detour. The three stood on the bottom slat of the gate and looked into the field. Nancy's head barely reached the top of the gate. She clung tight. "There they are!"

Three silhouettes moved softly in the grey: two adult ponies and a foal, all grazing. Nancy begged John for the sugar-lumps she had insisted they brought with them. She called. They stopped their grazing and looked in her direction for some time.

Slowly at first, then quickening their pace, the two adults began to move towards them, followed erratically by the foal. One pony was piebald, the other was brown and the foal was also brown. Their feet were muddy from the field where they lived, which had boggy patches despite the dry weather. The brown pony took a sugar lump from Nancy's proferred hand ("Ooh, you're squidgy!" she laughed, meaning its muzzle and tongue) while the other one snorted importantly. The foal was shy, and resisted Nancy's blandishments for a while, but was at last persuaded to accept a lump.

"They belong to the gypsies," explained John. "Whom the locals think are a great nuisance. They're always getting up petitions about them."

Eye: What do you think about them?

John: They don't bother me. They create far less shit than the town-planners.

Two or three caravans were parked at the other end of the field. They were modern, with a steel finish, but succumbing to rust. For some reason, a small mountain of blue plastic milk-bottle crates resided next to them, also a quantity of paint-cans. Resting on two paint-cans was a big portable cassette player. There was no sign of anybody.

Nancy: Do the ponies pull the caravans?

John: No, dear, they have cars nowadays. And bikes. (He pointed to a rusty child's bicycle leaning against one caravan.) You'd make a good gypsy, Eileen.

Eye: Perhaps that's what I am.

With difficulty, John prised Nancy away from the gate, and they continued on their way. The ponies followed them with their sad, unfathomable eyes until they were out of sight.

And now they were at the foot of the unmade lane that led to the house. An elderly man was walking briskly down, smoking a cigarette in the gloom, accompanied by a mongrel dog. He feigned not to notice them at first, then nodded curtly at John as he passed, thus honing down human contact to the barest minimum consistent with politeness. In passing, he threw Eye the quickest of stares. The dog began an exhaustive investigation of the ditch.

John nodded in response.

"I want a dog!" wailed Nancy.

"They're pretty snooty round here," John told Eye in a whisper.

They turned to wait for Nancy, who was gazing longingly at the dog.

As he turned the corner, the elderly neighbour discarded his cigarette. He disappeared then in the direction of the pub, followed by the dog. Night approached. It was surprising how dark it already was. The disintegrated cigarette sparks fled randomly over the dark road's surface before they too vanished.

•

So he had become a writer, then. She was on the front porch of the farmhouse, pumping up her tyres, cleaning the bicycle with a rag from her saddle-bag, oiling the gears, hubs and chain. Now and again she stopped to sip from the glass of wine that rested on the window-ledge.

Inside the house, he gazed thoughtfully at a blank computer screen, waiting. The blank ahead, wide blue nothingness, nothing there till you put it there. Vertigo, suddenly. To be without a name, and then to name the world, fix it down, limit its wide blue possibilities, and its new limits becoming your past, receding into memory. And still there's a blank ahead, the terror of the next moment, and yet wanting to be there.

She put the rag and the oilcan away, the smell a comfort. Dark out there in the garden. And chilly now. She shivered, glad that she wouldn't have to sleep outside tonight. He had not been a writer ... then, when she'd known him before. When had he become one? And what had he written? Had he written the story of her life? Had he mapped it out, and had she wiped it from her consciousness so she could return to haunt him with the inevitability of unknowable potential?

Every moment bang up against the unspeakable blank, uncertainty.

But then how to account for the accompanying certainty

that it's all there somewhere, on the brink, past present and future?

Closing the blue front door behind her, she crossed the kitchen, where the boiler was humming comfortably. Earlier she'd cleared away the lunch things here, enjoying its warmth. John had cooked them all a stew, unappreciated by Nancy, but welcome to Eye, whose appetite had briefly returned.

She went through to the living room, where she could hear the sound of voices. But there was only Nancy, slumped in an easy chair watching an unsuitable TV programme.

Eye smiled.

There was peace in this house. The living room was long and narrow with three leaded windows that gave out onto the garden and its greenish gloom. The walls were wood-panelled, and the floor was wood blocks, well worn to goldenness. Books and cushions served both as the room's main furnishing and its litter.

Leaving Nancy, who had not registered her presence, she carried her wine-glass, which needed refilling, up the stairs. Off the long landing were five doors. She knocked softly on the one opposite.

"Come in."

John was tapping at the keyboard in front of his computer screen, his face glowing because most of the room was dark. He turned and smiled briefly when she entered. She laid a hand lightly on his shoulder and watched for a little less than a minute before reaching for the bottle of wine which stood on the desktop, and refilling her glass.

The computer was different to the one she used at work. Its screen was a restful blue-grey, and John moved the pointer over it incessantly, using the mouse, which rested on its mouse-pad by his right hand. He would tap briskly, two-fingered, at the keyboard for some moments; then break to use the mouse to point somewhere else in the text; then go back to the keyboard.

Presently, Eye said: "My computer at work gave me a shock, yesterday morning."

John: A shock?

Eye: Yeah. That's why I, well, I took the rest of the day off.

John: That's very unusual.

Eye: It was like massive static. And I felt sick afterwards.

John: Are you sure? The flicker from the screen can trigger off fits, I'm told.

Eye: Is that right?

John: But you've never suffered from epilepsy, or anything like that, have you?

She was silent.

John: Perhaps feeling sick was a different thing. Did you complain? You should have them do something about it.

Eye: It's OK. I'm not going back anyway.

When had she decided this? In the moment of saying it? She tested its truth-value for some moments. Actually, she'd decided it in the washroom of the company building, it was just that she had never formulated it as desire (if it was desire).

John: Are you staying the night?

Eye (after a pause): If that's OK.

John: Do you want me to fix you up with fresh bedding in one of the bedrooms? You know, the others have gone for the weekend.

(No reply.)

As John continued working, she carried her wine-glass, now full, back down the stairs. Then she went into the living room. Nancy was still watching television. The moving colours from the TV screen played on the child's face, just as the steady blue from the computer had washed her father's.

"Is that alcohol?" asked the child, disapprovingly. And then, the disapproval vanishing suddenly, "Can I have a taste?"

"Just a sip," smiled Eye.

Nancy took a minute sip, and followed this with a grotesquely exaggerated grimace: "Yuk!"

Eye: I think your Daddy said you were to go to bed in a minute. What's this, the news? Are the children's programmes over?

Nancy: Can I have another taste of the alcohol?

The end of the news bulletin was approaching: "... police say the killer may have been able to dispose of clues ..."

Eye: Where's your Mummy?

Nancy: She's gone to America.

Eye: Will she come back?

Nancy: Yes, she'll come back soon.

Eye: Are you looking forward to that?

Nancy: Yes.

There was peace in this house, seductive peace. But it wasn't something she was part of. She was forever gazing upon it from outside, as if her true place was back among the rank shrubbery and fallen leaves of the garden, looking for a light in the locked house. Now she was playing the part of someone who had always lived in the house, who would always live there. But it was a trick, even if it was one in which both Nancy and her father, for reasons Eye didn't know, were for the moment colluding in. Yet the child had said she was looking forward to the return of her mother. What did that mean? I know what it means, thought Eye, it means: no future here. One way or another.

The two highly groomed women newscasters were beginning to relax into gentle badinage as the final, lighter items of news were mopped up.

"... scientists now believe the landmapping satellite that has been falling out of orbit will crash to earth in the early hours of tomorrow, our time. The fragments are likely to fall into the sea and are not expected to pose any danger ... and now for news of today's sport, over to ..."

•

"Something is always happening for the first and last time."

Why had she said that? thought John. What prompted the utterance, which appeared to arise out of nothing, out of no context? Occasionally, this kind of oracular message surfaced, as though it had been curled damply in the salt-encrusted neck of a bottle that had spent the past five years tossing in the swell on its voyage from an unknown country. As though it had not originated with her, but with her atavistic self, whatever that was. What was the matter with her? She wasn't like this before, surely?

Five years. Not a word from her. Not since Nancy was born. Well, she was never going to get on with Nancy's mother, was she? Just a change of address note every so often, always an inner city address, each clearly destined to be as temporary as the one before. Then, last week, the surprise. He'd sent the invitation as a matter of routine, naturally. And to come down from having put his daughter to bed, the house filling with conversation, to enter the kitchen and to find her there suddenly, awkwardly, in a black skirt and white blouse, making conversation with someone, who was it, that woman, the art editor, and her dark face just exactly the same as ever, with a slant of late sunlight across it, screwed with concentration because she couldn't hear properly what was being said, because there was a classic soul track playing, someone had turned the stereo up too loud too soon and it was crashing into the kitchen, well it was bound to cause a little leap of the heart, even now; and he going: What are you doing here? and she turning, a wry smile: Well, you did invite me, and this time I came. And he: Sorry, don't let me interrupt (to the art director, who senses something, and moves away to fill her glass), and then to her, after the usual awkward silence: Well, what are you up to? Oh, I'm squatting, she goes, draining her own glass in one gulp, nervous, he supposes, she knows nobody here. Squatting, eh? Yeah, three of us, three girls, it's a great house, not as good as this, though, I want to have a look at your garden before it gets dark. Sure — and there's some halting chat about the garden — then, Do you want another drink? and just then of course he's interrupted, some other people have brought their baby, he has to organise an undisturbed place for it to sleep in its carry-cot, and by the time he gets back to the kitchen she's disappeared; and later he sees her standing on her own in the far corner of the long living room, another drink in her hand, eyes closed and moving her slender hips slowly to the record that's now playing. But by now it's filling up, and she's at the other end of the room; what he wants to do is go up to her quietly and speak her name, so that she opens her eyes and smiles her rare smile; and try and continue the conversation beyond the platitudinous opening gambits if possible, but he has to weave through a crowd in a small space, one or two of whom accost him cheerfully attempting to tell him a would-be witty and far from amusing anecdote about the difficulty they had finding the place by car, so that by the time he gets to the other side she's vanished, and he wonders if he just imagined her standing there. And the third and last time he sees her it's only for an instant, going out the back door which has been left open for the air and for the convenience of those who wish to inspect the garden, before it gets dark, naturally, which it almost is, her small and almost vulnerable figure in its short skirt, there and gone. OK, I'll talk to her when she comes in again, he thinks. But the evening wears on, wine gets spilled, before you know it people start looking for their coats, it's not like it used to be a few years ago and suddenly it's thinning out and she's not there. He asks someone: Oh, I think she got a lift home, she didn't look well, had a bit too much to drink. Shit. You're kidding. You're kidding.

Suddenly, just for a moment, vertigo assailed him; his whole body tightened. But soon it was OK again.

He reached over the bed and tugged the small cord, which instantly flooded the covers with light. The glow reached her, finally; she stood on the other side of the room framed in the window, gazing outside, across the overgrown garden, and beyond, too. Silver also touched her face from this direction: a moon had risen, and was jostling with the moving clouds.

Yes, a gypsy. Especially in this light. Her small oval face, darkening, her dark hair, glistening. And she so seldom smiled, but when she did it was a rare brilliance. That funny little twist of her lips, the white teeth.

But what did she mean, about first and last times? It didn't bode well, whatever it was.

Eye said: "Can I have a bath?"

"Yes, of course."

He switched on the radio and undressed slowly, while slow jazz played, interspersed with idle chat: "…and maybe you've got a funny story or two to tell about your DIY disaster. The phone lines are now open.…" Finally, he got into bed naked, pulled the cord that plunged him into darkness and lay there listening to the music. In the next room he could hear his daughter Nancy sighing in her sleep, as she so often did; close at hand, the radiator creaking; and further off, down the passage, muffled sounds of water. At last, these swelled into a rushing gurgle. Footsteps in the passage. The door squeaked open slowly.

Eye dropped onto the floor the towel that swaddled her and got into bed beside him. He could feel her small naked breasts squashed up against his side briefly. Fresh soap smell. He put an arm round her, and she moved her head to accommodate this. With his other hand he switched off the radio, and they were in silence as well as darkness.

She trembled. Are you cold, he said, but she didn't reply.

Presently, she spoke. She said: "Nancy's mother…"

"That's difficult. I don't know what's going to happen, after she comes back from America. I haven't said anything to Nancy. But she must know. It's going to be difficult for her."

"Yes."

The moon came in at the open window. The satellite smashed into the city, causing horror and devastation, millions dead or injured. But that was miles away. She shut her eyes tight to keep from waking.

About three in the morning, John woke in a sweat of desire, his erect penis brushing against Eye's thigh. She was breathing slowly and easily. Sleepily, he moved his hand over her left breast. She moaned slightly in her dream. He kissed her hair, trailing his hand lightly down over her flattened belly. Minutes passed.

She had kept her knickers on, he noticed. He moved his hand over her crotch, rubbing gently. There was wadding there. So she was having a period then. That meant it was safe.

Gently, he began removing the knickers, rolling them down

her thighs. There was something curious about the sanitary napkin, which seemed to fan out and fall to pieces.

He moved on top of her. She did not stir, or cry.

She was awake now, but felt nothing. His hardness said nothing to her either way. Neither desire nor revulsion. Not even when he was kissing her mouth, forcing her lips open with his tongue.

And finally, with difficulty, he was in her, and moving in slow rhythm. She remained motionless, only flinching slightly once, when he touched the bruising on her inner thigh, her legs stretched out and her arms at her sides, not responding, just waiting. Not tensed, but waiting for it to be over. The rhythm quickened, he shuddered once and became quiet.

He kissed her eyes. There was wetness there.

"What's the matter?"

She shook her head, but it was too dark to interpret this gesture.

As he rolled over, his hand encountered what he thought was the sanitary napkin that had felt so odd. He clenched his fist over it and brought it up out of the covers. It was part of a wad of banknotes.

The bed was littered with more banknotes. Frowning, he switched on the light. She blinked, knitting her brow.

They were high denominations, and a lot of them.

John: Where did you get this money?

Eye: From a bank.

John: Oh, very funny. What on earth was it doing ... there? (He started collecting the rest of the notes and depositing them on the side shelf.)

Eye: Just switch off the light, please, John, and go to sleep.

Once more, they were in darkness. The moon seemed to have disappeared again.

(Silence. Then the distant rumble of a freight train.)

Peace. Too much peace.

John: Will you be going in the morning?

Eye: I have to, John. I'm sorry.

Good morning, you lucky people, said the robin. You don't deserve such pampering! Oh, what a beautiful. And now here's a tune, I say, from my friend the chaffinch. Hmm. Spoon into the. Square light. From a whisper to a roar. Glorious whisper. Sunday morning. Get up.

With a spoon, she squeezes the tea-bag against the side of the mug, then hunts. Something in the way she moves. No other lover. Flap.

Oh, pussy. How could you.

There is a balm in Gilead. Slurps. Kitchen towel, quick. Not a sound. Not a mouse in the house. Here is the farming news.

No blame. No sound. No catch. No way. No footfall, hearken, on the stair. No ground. For suspicion. He mustn't hear. No dreams. No good.

Opens the fridge, frosted milk is extracted, the suddenness of its light startles, and the jerk is a trigger too, changes silence into hum. The cat says yes, please. Slam. Where's that bowl, here it is. Love it, lap it, good.

The portable radio. On the fridge. Old-fashioned. Another memory struggles, and gives up. Just like home. Where was that?

It's going to be another warm day, temperatures high for the time of year, but yesterday's winds will return, and towards evening there will be rain on the south coast.

Chinese notebook. On the table. She writes, with a stubby pencil, watched. By the cat. Hey pussy pussy.

No fox.

The sun begins to gild the far posts. Rhododendron bushes wait. Holly prickles. A tiny rodent through the undergrowth. Rustles.

Her slim brown hand, bangled, writes. Nobody else about yet. Tears the page out. Leaves it on the table. Pink checks.

Cough. Buzz. The boiler roars into life, from a whisper. Radiators begin to clank. Thank you. That was chaffinch there, and here's a segue into blackbird. Take it away, kid. Bye bye. Memories come back to haunt you. Blow.

Click.

Drinks from a steaming mug, slowly. Takes it from room to room. He was still asleep when she slid out. Made a small, hopeless noise. Rumpled to bits. Reached, but did not find.

The money! Paper notes on the bedside shelf. Put them in the shoulder bag. Strap it. Poor John, oblivious.

And in the other bedroom the child, rosily asleep too.

The living room. Sun streams here, and the tiny dust particles hold hands. Off they go now. Through the leaded windows, hippety hop. Green/gold stream. Scatter books. The television, opaque at last, a golden picture of the window on its.

Porcelain sunburst in the bathroom. Really must change. Green in here, too. Swiss cheese. Rubber. Hanging spider. Succulent. She presses the lever, and water rushes.

Doesn't want to go. But the inexorable. Shadows on the path. Squeak. Bats in the loft?

Warm already. She is on the front porch, stuffing her coat behind the saddle-bag, held by an elasticated strap, the shoulder bag too. Short-sleeved. Adjusts the blue scarf, and ties it. Below her chin.

Shuts the front door gently.

Wheels the bicycle towards the iron gate.

•

Eye cycled slowly, bumpily, down to the main road, where the tarmac began. It was a pristine morning, populated as yet only by the invisible birds. The road shone with early sunlight. No traffic in sight. Though there was the sound of a radio, or something, somewhere.

She turned left, changed gear, and began to build to a

steady speed. On her left was the hedge that bounded the farmhouse garden, then the field holding the ponies. On her right, a scruffy expanse of common ground, grass worn bare in patches, its space defined by glinting items of litter: silver foil from cigarette packets, bent cans and bottle shards; and its farthest boundaries delimited by a row of shops: a laundrette, a newsagent's (both already open for trade), and the shop where she had bought last night's bottle of wine, now shuttered.

She couldn't see the ponies as she passed the field, but the road twisted round to take her close by the gypsy encampment. The rusty caravans were still there. A dark man in a stained sweatshirt was sitting on an upturned milk crate. In his thirties, perhaps, his chin covered by stubble that was even now making the transition into the category of beard. He was listening to loud, heavily distorted pop music from the cassette player next to him. He watched her all the way. It was a gaze of indifference, as foreign to hostility as to solidarity. She thought: It's the same gaze as the ponies last night. If I had the equivalent of a sugar-lump, why, he would come over and take it. Since I don't, he leaves me alone.

The blueness of the sky began to deepen. Only wispy cloud.

Now there were prefabricated huts by the side of the road, each with its own special garden, the metal of some alleviated by climbing roses. Ahead was the sliproad for the motorway. She wanted to avoid that. So she started bearing right. Signalling. Where to?

The future beckoned.

Both John and Nancy had been asleep in the respective bedrooms when she left. Soon, perhaps, Nancy would awake, and come padding downstairs in her night-dress, in search of breakfast television. Perhaps she would find the note on the table, and take it up to her father's room for him to read, bleary-eyed. By then, Eye would be miles away. What if Nancy had found her there, in her father's bed? But she had said she'd be up before any of them. What she hadn't said was she would be away. Of course she felt bad about this, but there was no alternative; her weakness for the simple everyday pleasures would have bogged her there, when her journey's imperative, the pull of the future, was all that really mattered, was all that was vital, in the sense of pure survival, or the information crucial to survival. So it wasn't a case of waiting on the next moment after all, there was a choice to be made, no getting away from that. And the pain it might bring, at least in the short term. At least, that was a discovery.

The prefabricated huts gave way to more fields, in the distance of which several animals were content to remain, and these in turn to a more extensive housing estate. The tenements were of the same ugly, blocky design, or rather, non-design, that she had seen before, their windows too small proportionately for the size of the walls, whose concrete lower regions were the canvas for inscrutable graffiti in black and primary colours. Each block had a common front door, painted deep red, except for one, where in place of the door was corrugated iron. Plywood covered the windows of this building, and one upper window had a halo of black soot round it. The road threaded its way through the estate. Its backdrop was the high, grey-green ridge, fringed with yellowing trees, that she knew was the beginning of Cuckoo Wood.

Only one human here. A small boy in a tracksuit, who had been kicking a ball by himself against the wall of one of the blocks, stopped to shout something incomprehensible at her as she passed.

The ground began to shimmer. Yellow ragwort profusely grew among oily stains. Dandelions nodded in the slight breeze. She felt at peace, and moreover the peace was unmixed with that sense of constriction she had felt last night, in the house, and about which she had suffered such guilt, because there was no reason to feel this, no reason whatsoever, she had imposed herself on John's hospitality after all, he had not behaved badly. Perhaps it was the tension of having to play a part, underlying that seductive peace. That must have been it. To play a part in the drama that was being put together minute by minute, and to not be able to fall back on a full repertoire of responses. To not be able to fall back on, to trust fully what happened, to insure herself against the excess of possibilities. So the choice to leave had definitely been the right one. But was she then obliged to continue her gypsy-like existence, outside of engagement and human interaction?

The question was too difficult; easier to pedal, one push at a time, one leg and then the other, building up a journey from such small blocks of attention: a voyage of discovery? or invention? Each small focusing of attention contributed to the big focusing, the world coming together.

Then its meaning would begin to come behind it.

Already far below and to the left now snaked the motorway, populated with the first vestiges of Sunday traffic. She was distancing herself from it, yard by yard, seeking the secondary road. Where to? South.

The bicycle creaked in a good rhythm. The handlebars felt solid under her knuckles. Her beloved machine, well oiled and cleaned, would take her to the end of all possibilities.

Actually, she wasn't sure of the route. The road was unfamiliar, but the general direction was good. So keep going, Eye, she told herself.

Although with every push on the pedal she was distancing herself from the heart of the big city, the metropolis was not going to give up without a struggle. The open countryside beckoned, but it was a promise that was never fulfilled. (She almost began to feel sympathy for John, and his quest for a rural idyll.) Each time an open field threatened to interpose its undulation of yellow and green and its scent of flowering and decay, a vegetative island as Cuckoo Wood had been, the city fought back: with a garage, a petrol station, a supermarket, a housing estate. And so the dialectic continued. Money's aura wafted from some of the houses, which were set back imposingly from the road behind trim hedges, ivy-clad, adorned by big gleaming parked cars; then round the next bend they would be newer, boxier, poorer. Next to that would be a stretch of wasteland, or a used car lot, or a dump.

The sun climbed in the sky, and the clouds melted quietly away to allow it centre stage. Eye's moving shadow grew both blacker and shorter.

She was beginning to feel faint, and sick. She stopped, and got off. She rested under the shade of a garage wall, propping the bike against it and sitting on a ledge. Why the sudden weakness?

But gradually it passed. She was thirsty. The saddle-bag contained the bottle of orange juice, now half empty, that she had bought the evening before last in the city. It was warm, but served to slake her parched tongue. Soon she felt well enough to continue.

At one point she hit the fossil of an abandoned railway. Where its tracks had once lain was now a cinder footpath, flanked by grassy verges, the cinders bearing the imprint of boots, training shoes and horses' hooves. Occasionally there were horses' droppings, dried in the sun. Eye's bicycle wheels carved a silent trajectory through the soft blackness. The track went through what had once been a station. The platforms reared on either side and hugged the path through a long curve. They were overgrown with weeds and even bushes on top, but had been faced with new brick, some of which was already coming away. Detached houses with untidy gardens backed onto the former railway; from one, Eye could hear the sound of a vacuum cleaner. A child's bike, minus one wheel, had been flung onto the cinders; she had to swerve to avoid it. Beside a broken wall an enamelled cast-iron bath, complete with taps, had been abandoned. Further on was the charred frame of what had once been a settee. Already weeds were growing through the black springs.

The footway came to an end, and she rejoined the main road.

An hour or two went by.

A railway was sweeping towards her. A real one this time. The rusting tracks branched into a marshalling yard whereon stood a few forlorn trucks and vans coupled together in the heat, manufacturers' logos faded on their sides. One line branched away to follow an embankment which led it to a steel girder bridge above the road. Only sporadic traffic was using the road, but Eye preferred to follow a wide footpath which parallelled it, beginning to slope down and separately duck under the railway. She freewheeled down the slope, which burrowed between concrete embankments on either side of it.

The bicycle gathered speed as it approached the underpass. Overhead, a slow shunting engine was crossing, clanking. In the distance glittered the multiplied windows of several multi-storey ferroconcrete office buildings. Eye began to feel mounting excitement. She actually closed her eyes as she freewheeled.

She felt she was approaching the future.

Why did she feel this?

Afterwards, she couldn't have said. But there was an element of a child's game about it: she decided the bridge marked the turning point between present and future; once under it and up the other side she would have arrived, she would have made the jump in time, she would be in the future. It was something that, simply, occurred to her. The other side of the railway bridge was the world of the future.

The shadow of the bridge made its mark on her for a brief moment.

Then she was through, her momentum carrying her free-wheeling up the slope. Into the future!

In the future the sun was even more brilliant than it had been. It was just as she had anticipated: she had an exhilarating sense of being on the planet as she sped, on the blue ball of it, beneath a blue limitless sky that offered every possibility that space could promise. Was that futuristic? Yes, she thought. It was nothing to do with crystal domes and computers. It was a sense that the future moment had arrived, without turning instantly into a less than adequate present, or, already by the time you'd had the thought, into the past. Another word for it, of course, was magic. The link between the world of appearances and her presence in that world. Had she been more alert, she might have sensed before she did, before it was too late, that something was wrong, that perhaps one of the things that gave the scene its futuristic aspect was the absence of others, the lack of people, the magnificent loneliness of it all, as prophesied by the boy in the all-night petrol station; she alone had burst into its brilliance because ships of unknown metal had transported everyone she might have recognised to inconceivably distant stars, abandoning these half-cities to the rust and dust and the return of nature. However, in her instant pleasure she ignored this. The sun's benevolence shone on the whole scene. The entire landscape, railway marshalling yard, sheds with their rust encroaching, a dump of what looked like discarded electronic parts, distant office blocks, elm trees behind the road, ragwort and perhaps wild thyme reclaiming the cracks among the concrete, all these things which were perfectly ordinary and might as well have belonged to the day-to-day, all were transfigured under that golden sun.

But it was too brilliant to be the sun. As she emerged from under the bridge and up the slope, it too was moving. It was getting bigger and brighter. Moving towards her, towards the earth. It wasn't the sun, it was something moving towards the earth, and burning as it came.

Her momentum was beginning to be spent, and there was still some stretch of upward slope to go. The bicycle was slowing. So she stepped on the pedal. At once there was a terrific bang.

•

There was a terrific bang.

•

Smells were something she remembered. Fresh tarmac, soot and oil, and something pleasantly like honeysuckle. Sounds, too. The protesting groan of the shunting engine's gearing, as it passed on the bridge overhead. The gurgle of water. Someone shouting in the distance. A dog barking.

These were the scents and sounds of the world of the future.

She also had a confused impression of a big silver wheel, spinning furiously and flashing in the sun as it spun. Angels in shining space-suits were calling to her on special radio frequencies she could hear inside her head. Their voices had a kind of warble about them, as though they had adapted the language of the birds. They echoed in her bone structure and musculature.

But what were they saying to her?

Two angels were coming towards her, out of the bright wheel. They were riding silver bicycles through the solid air, and signalling furiously to her, making quick circular movements with their right index fingers. As they approached, she saw without surprise they were Dee and Zoo, clad in silver lamé. She understood that the movement of their fingers exactly matched the spinning of the brilliant wheel, and she understood too the necessity of getting in synchrony with that spin.

Dee and Zoo came up to Eye. Without dismounting from their air bicycles, each gently took hold of one shoulder. They began to spin her around. Faster and faster she went, the world of the future becoming a blur; she was approaching the speed of light and then suddenly there was darkness.

Hello, she called out, where are you? Dee? Zoo? Are you there?

As her eyes became accustomed to the gloom, she began to see that she was in a passage, narrow and gently curving. She thought she could detect a faint hum. She thought it came from the direction she was facing, where the passage curved to the left. So she began to move in that direction.

As soon as she started walking, she became aware of another sound, this time behind her. Pattering footsteps. She stopped, and the sound stopped. She began walking again, and it started. Was it an echo of her own footsteps? No, the rhythm was different, and there was a definite time lag, though just a second, between her stopping and starting and the sound's stopping and starting.

She took a few paces back. All of a sudden, she could discern a small black shape. Two points of light briefly glowed, reflecting what ambient light there was filtered through this passage.

A small dog. It meant no harm, she knew. It would protect her if it could. She smiled, turned back and went on.

The passage continued to curve leftward. But somehow she intuited that it was not simply going round in a circle. Each step she took was fresh, at no point did she re-tread old ground. The passage was spiralling inward, to the heart. Of what? Of the satellite.

Ghostly voices began to mingle with the hum, which was becoming louder. At intervals, the passage was interrupted by a circular open doorway, through which she stepped. She knew the dog was following her.

At last, she came to a doorway that was blocked up. With increasing excitement, she realised that she had arrived at the "heart". On the other side, she could hear the voices swell till they sounded like rain sweeping through a forest.

She turned to the dog, which was several yards behind her. Stay, she whispered. Obediently, it sat down on its haunches, gazing at her, its tongue lolling.

She touched the metal door, which slid open, and stepped through.

•

(The auditorium, which is full, breaks out into enthusiastic applause as Eye appears and begins to walk down the steps towards the stage at the centre of the three-quarter-circle of banked seats. Dee and Zoo, in their silver space costumes, are waiting near the stage to greet her.)

Dee (grinning broadly): Eye! This is your moment. On you go.

Zoo: You are looking terrific!

Eye (perplexed): What do you mean? I look a mess. What?

(They help her onto the stage, where a replica of her bicycle, embalmed in chrome, is mounted. She sees that she is expected to sit on this, and does so. The applause swells again, then hushes as the house lights dim and one spotlight focuses on Eye. She blinks.)

Eye: What's happening?

(Another spotlight snaps on. It picks out a woman in late

middle age. Her grey hair, straggly and parted in the middle, appears to have been lavishly treated with ashes from a long dead hearth, so that it looks even more ghastly. She wears a shapeless costume of hessian that reaches below her knees; her feet are bare and filthy with mud. In either hand, she holds a full plastic carrier bag printed with the logo of a familiar super-market. It is the Miserable Woman. She shuffles towards the stage.)

The Miserable Woman: War! Rumours of War!

Eye: Oh. I know you.

(The Miserable Woman mounts the steps to the stage. She puts down her carrier bags and confronts Eye, pointing.)

The Miserable Woman: Why do you hate me? I haven't done nothing wrong to you.

Eye (shifting on the static bicycle): I don't hate you.

The Miserable Woman: Don't make it worse by lying. Little girls shouldn't lie.

Eye: You were in the art gallery, weren't you? I was looking for you afterwards, I wanted to say I was sorry if I was rude. There was a bridge, with homeless people sleeping under it, I saw a figure, I thought it was you and I called out. But it wasn't. So I left a message instead. Did you get it?

The Miserable Woman (ignoring her): Is it because I'm weak? I have funny turns, you know.

Eye: I remember. There's nothing wrong with my memory!

The Miserable Woman: Is it because I'm a victim? Is it because I'm a victim of society what is so unfair to a poor woman like me what has no home to go to?

Eye (upset): Maybe I hated you once. I don't now. I'm sorry. That's what I'm trying to say.

The Miserable Woman (with evil glint in her previously expressionless pale eyes): Is it because I'm you? Because you see yourself in me, you weak stupid girl with no memory?

(Eye bows her head. Her knuckles whiten on the handle-bars.)

The Miserable Woman (bringing her palms together): Holy, holy, holy!

117

(Eye looks up, abruptly.)

Eye: I know what you mean. I couldn't help thinking about that while I was riding through the night. After I met you in the art gallery. And then again later, this morning, if you can still say that. I don't know whether it's still this morning. Maybe that was eight hundred thousand years ago. Anyway. I think you mean the unknown, a hole in our present knowledge. When I showed you those three pictures in the art gallery you said holy, holy, holy, which meant you saw three holes, or three unknowns. Which was another way of saying, well, the sacred, if you like. Or even the future?

The Miserable Woman (even more dolorously): Holy, holy, holy!

(There is a loud multiple howling of electronic sirens, and bright blue lights flash on and off. On to the stage, coming from all directions, roar seven police motorcycles with heavily visored riders, wearing the aspect of angels in a holy war. They screech to a stop just short of Eye and the Miserable Woman. Their radios are all broadcasting different, almost incomprehensible messages at once. The Miserable Woman has closed her eyes and remains immobile. Eye looks around her, alarmed. Two policemen in checked caps materialise, loom over her, one a weasel-like Bad Policeman, the other a large, sad-eyed Good Policeman.)

The Good Policeman (to Eye): Is this lady troubling you, madam?

Eye (nervous): No ... no.

The Bad Policeman (to the Miserable Woman): OK, you're coming with us.

The Miserable Woman: Rumours of War! Holy, holy, holy!

The Bad Policeman (to Eye): You'll have to make a statement of course.

The Good Policeman: Yeah, a statement is required, madam.

Eye (indignantly): I don't want to make any statement.

The Bad Policeman: I'm afraid there's no alternative, madam. Unless you want to be charged with obstructing the police in carrying out their duties.

Eye: I have nothing to say. Please go away, and leave this poor woman alone.

The Good Policeman: Come on madam, this won't take long, I'm sure you have plenty to say, which will be very helpful to us.

Eye: What? About what?

The Good Policeman (surprised): About everything! I hope you weren't planning on leaving anything out. That could constitute, if I may say so, a serious offence.

Eye: OK, try this, this is my statement: "Please go away, and leave this poor woman alone."

The angel/police motorcycles: Er, stern rumours alpha romeo please. We're ingesting pap, ruinously, can you copy? Slip the junction, breakfasts all over, believed heading parsimoniously chic. Rogue queen in the vicinity, er, zen dogs in haste. Do you read urine, delta? Roger, file down the house, er, muddle it, no, repeat, puddle it. Slaves have wept, no sign alpha romeo. Say again. Beep. Now squinting through a hot wasteland, apprehended darlings, repeat, darklings. Do you read? (Etc, ad lib)

The Bad Policeman: I'm afraid that will not be considered adequate in a court of law, madam, and I must advise you ... (coming closer to Eye) ... wait a minute, wait a minute, what have we here?

(He takes out a torch and shines it in her eyes, making her squint and tighten her grip on the handlebars. He puts it away and turns to the Good Policeman.)

The Bad Policeman: Well, well, what have we here, John? It's the same young lady.

The Good Policeman: Right you are, John.

The Bad Policeman: Well, madam ... (giving the word unnecessary emphasis) ... you may not wish to give a statement at this point in time, whichever point of time it may be, but I seem to remember a little matter of giving a false name, is that right? What was that name again, a certain ... (makes big show of consulting notebook) ... ah yes, Mrs Sonia Newman, now this is very interesting, are you trying to tell us something?

Eye: I don't know anything about that person, whoever she is.

The Good Policeman (sorrowfully): It really would be much easier and save all of us an awful lot of trouble, madam, if you gave a statement. Just get it off your chest. You'll feel much better.

The Bad Policeman (menacingly): What exactly is it you're trying to tell us?

Eye: Just get off my back!

The Bad Policeman: Well, John, it looks like the young lady isn't going to co-operate.

The Good Policeman: It looks that way, John.

The Bad Policeman: OK, don't go away, madam, we'll get back to you once we've cleared up this other business.

(He strides back to the Miserable Woman.)

The angel/police motorcycles: Slovenly appurtenances (beep). Request permission slide same into relevant arseholes, er, over. Syllogism in rags, believed proceeding up shit creek, dialectic unknown, shall we pursue, Roger?

The Miserable Woman (frightened): Holy!

The Good Policeman: Never mind that, come along with us darling, it's for your own good.

(Each policeman grasps the Miserable Woman by one arm.)

The Miserable Woman (suddenly raising her voice to a scream and pointing at Eye): It was her! She's the one!

The Bad Policeman: OK, shut it. Are you going to come quietly?

Eye (upset): Leave her alone!

The Miserable Woman: She's the one!

(Suddenly, wriggling free of the policemen, she scoops up a plastic carrier bag in each hand. She upturns them. Instead of the expected rubbish, they are filled with thousands of banknotes, which now flutter out in great squalls, filling the space of the stage like a blizzard. Also mingled with ashes from the woman's hair, which begin to pour out. A wind starts up from nowhere and helps to whip the banknotes and ashes around. Howling. Unbearable.)

The Miserable Woman: Money! Money! Money from the future!

(The blizzard subsides and the money and ashes begin to flutter down and settle on the floor. The policemen pick the Miserable Woman up bodily and carry her kicking and screaming offstage. The motorcycles rev up with a deafening roar, perform tight circles in unison and vanish into the wings, their blue lights flashing. Actually, wings is a misnomer; it seems to Eye that they return whence they came, that is, out of the seven corners of the earth, the sacred distance. Lights go down again. Short pause. Then the Good Policeman comes back, kicking piles of banknotes aside.)

The Good Policeman: Very sorry about that, madam.

Eye: My God! John! It's you! (And sure enough, it isn't the policeman at all, but John wearing his black bobble hat.)

John: Eileen!

(Eye gets off the bicycle, they rush to each other and embrace. Audience applause. General lighting.)

John: How are you? Are you OK?

Eye: Yes. I think so. Are you in the future, then? I never thought the future would be like this.

(A dark figure casts his shadow on the stage. Eye whips round.)

Eye: Who's that?

The dark figure: It's not we who are in the future. It's you who are in the past.

Eye (scared): What d'you mean? Who are you? Are you the other policeman?

(He enters a spotlight. But it isn't the Bad Policeman, after all. He has dark, neatly brushed hair and is wearing a white shirt and tie and a lightweight business suit. Confused, Eye retreats to her bicycle as though for comfort and remounts.)

Eye: I know you. Your name is John. You're John, too!

(John 2 approaches, smiling. He lifts one of Eye's hands off the handlebar and touches it briefly to his lips.)

John 2: Confusing, isn't it?

John: Just a minute. Who exactly are you?

(John 2 spots a chair at the rear of the stage, walks over to it slowly, takes his jacket off and drapes its over its back. Then he returns.)

John 2 (still smiling): Ask her.

John: Eileen?

Eye (agitated): I … I can't remember. It was a long time ago. Before the future began.

John 2: You didn't treat me very nicely.

Eye: I don't remember anything.

John 2: Holy, holy, holy, eh? It doesn't mean the unknown hole of the future. It means your memory is ineffective. There's a hole in it, or if you prefer, it isn't whole.

John: What's going on? Is this some kind of joke?

John 2: You see, Eileen — may I call you Eileen? — your project is a failure, after all. You decided to follow your instinct and let it lead you into the future. And you thought you had succeeded. But it hasn't brought you to the future at all. Instead, it has revealed to you your past. The past you were desperately trying to escape. There's no way you can escape from it.

John: Is this true, Eileen? Who is this guy?

Eye: Nothing to do with you.

John 2: There's more to her than meets the eye, if you'll pardon the joke. There's the secret Eye that you know nothing about. That she can't tell you about, but then that's normal for her, whoever she is. Who is she? Why, she's a different person in each situation. Aren't you?

(Dee, unable to contain herself any longer, jumps onto the stage, still in her silver angel suit.)

Dee: You bastard! Who are you to talk to her like that, anyway? (She is instantly restrained by Zoo, who pulls her back and whispers to her.)

Eye (stoutly): We're all like that, to some extent.

John 2 (faintly amused): What's that again?

Eye: We all play a part, depending on who we're with. There's nothing unusual in that. What's the point you're trying to make?

John 2: Ah yes, but we don't all compartmentalise our lives to quite that degree, do we, so that we're actually different people, to the extent that we don't even remember who we were? Heh? Makes a problem when it all has to come together.

Eye: What about you? (Suddenly confident.) You have a wife, don't you? I've seen her picture. I suppose you don't act differently with her? I suppose you've told her all about me?

Dee (excitedly, offstage): That's it, Eye, you've got him there!

John: Wife? You mean he's married?

John 2 (turning smoothly on him): Hmm. You're a nice one to talk.

John (primly): My wife and I have no secrets from each other. She's in America, that's all. Anyway, the thing is, what right have you to abuse Eileen?

John 2 (mock surprise): Abuse her? (To Eye:) Have I abused you, my darling? Or did you abuse me? I can't recall. (Momentary flash superimposed, everything whited out, auditorium fades to white on white, a huge image fills the space, a naked corpse of a young man on a mortuary slab or similar, viewed from the soles of the feet, picked out in light and shade; every few moments a violent spasm ripples through the body. The convulsions gradually become fewer and less violent. Just as suddenly, the image is wiped.)

Eye (covering her face with her hands in horror): I'm sorry … I'm sorry.

John: Don't apologise to him. I tell you what your chief fault is. Your anxiety to please everybody.

Eye (unhappily): Yes.

John 2: There you are, your friend John is right for once. Isn't he? In fact, you've even proved him right by agreeing with him. How neat.

Eye: What do you mean?

John 2: You have this tendency to agree with people, to mould your personality to fit in with whoever you're with. It works, because people don't notice it in isolation. They just think you're in tune with them.

John: Actually, they like you because you reflect their self-image.

John 2: Something like that, though I'd have it shorn of that woolly psychological jargon, personally. And even your body language changes. With me, you're, shall we say, more physical. Anyway, it begins to break down when all the bits of your life come together. You can't handle it then.

Dee (offstage): I hate to say it, but they're right. Up to a point. Don't let them use it. You're far too compliant, I've always said so, kid.

Eye: What is this anyway, a trial?

John 2: It's a show trial. Do you know what that means? It's when justice isn't necessarily done but is *seen* to be done. And guess who's on trial? Why, you are. Whoever you are. Let's face it, you're a blank slate, aren't you? The future? I can write any future I like on you.

Eye: I'm not going to even bother to reply to that.

John: That's unfair. Eileen is struggling for her vision of the future. She has a perfect right to do that. Even though we have our disagreements, I still defend her right...

John 2: Oh Christ almighty, hark at the patronising liberal!

John: Listen a minute. Eileen wants things to be different. The trouble is ...

John 2: The trouble is, she has no understanding of how the world really is, she's got this naive idea ...

John: No, no, the trouble is she has no political programme. She wants to change the world, but she has no idea how to go about it.

Dee (sotto voce): They're just as bad as each other, aren't they? Basically they're both just cops. Mind cops. They're both The Filth....

Zoo (also whispering): Shut up, it iss not finished.

John 2 (ironically): And you have?

John: I'm not saying I have all the answers. Maybe I once thought I did. But weariness takes over. Lately I've come down to thinking, there's very little we can do after all to change the world. Except work on the quality of our personal relationships.

I mean, I'm willing to admit I'm just as guilty in my way of, er, laying my strictures on Eileen.... (John 2 smiles and shakes his head pityingly, as though saying "See? just what I meant".) Well, what's wrong with that? It's all a question of give and take, isn't it? She and I get on just fine. Eileen, did we or did we not have a great time yesterday? And you got on superbly with Nancy ...

John 2 (to the audience): That's the orphan child.

John: ... and she liked you, she told me herself. What I mean is, we're, essentially, in harmony, and of course, that means conflict too, creative tension...

John 2 (snorting with laughter): Here it comes. Some proposal from the ageing hippie. He's so addled he's actually forgotten he's already married too.

John (angrily): Wait a minute, how come you claim to know so much about me?

(Pause.)

John 2 (brightly): It's because I'm dead. She killed me. Oh, didn't she tell you? The dead can see everything, you know. You can't see them, except in the future of course, but they can see right into your mind.

Eye: Dead? Listen, you don't even exist!

(Audience laughter.)

John 2 (urbanely): That's a nice cop-out, my dear.

John: OK, I'm going to proceed on that premise, that you don't exist, because that seems to be the only civilised way. To get back to what I was saying. Eileen, real life is full of conflict. And real relationships. That's where the politics of the possible starts. It's not some kind of lovey-dovey peace on earth no-hassle thing I'm talking about. And what you and I have, it's difficult, but it's real. All I'm saying is, your idea of Eden may not be the same as mine...

John 2: Not Eden.

John: What's that?

John 2: You talk about a real relationship but you don't even understand what she's saying. Eden is in the past. That's where you belong. Eileen, give her credit at least, is looking to the future.

Eye: Not your future. I don't want your future.

John 2: Placing the earthly paradise, not in the past, but in the future, makes it less an object of nostalgia, rather one of desire.

Dee (offstage, ironically): Oh, very good.

John 2: Am I right?

Eye (grudgingly): Something like that.

John 2: And you know all about desire, don't you, darling?

Eye (scornfully): I'm not falling for that one. You're despicable.

John 2: Just joking.

Eye: No, you're not.

John (who has squatted cross-legged on the floor): That's the spirit. Challenge the sexist bastard. Actually, I think I recognise him now. Of course. Why didn't I see it before? The guy nobody knew. At the party. Of course. Hovering on the fringes. Nobody seemed to know who he was or who had invited him. I gave it no thought. Then he disappeared. Come to think of it, so did you. It's my fault, I shouldn't have allowed you to ...

Eye: As for you, what's all this about allowing me to do this that or the other? You're just as bad in your way.

John (injured tone): How come?

Eye: He thinks of me as a sex object. But you want me to be a different kind of object, I don't know, an ideal of woman or something. You actually disapprove of me because I don't buy your pessimism about the world. About how the world's going. Yes, about the future. I don't play the role you think women should play. That means being permanently afraid. Staying in that one place. That's the role you secretly want women to play. Afraid of, what, poisons being injected into my body, weapons being trained on me, of nature (which women are supposed to be part of but men not), of nature dying, when really nature is more alive than you are. You look around you and you just project your pessimism, which is really your guilt feelings about yourself, onto the world. But you don't see the world as it really is, without you. It doesn't care about your guilt feelings. It'll get along without you, no problem. All your talk about being in harmony, you don't know what being in harmony is, you secretly just want your view to prevail. But that's not what you want to hear me say. It makes you feel better if I give in, and admit I'm a victim … oh, it's really convenient, isn't it? To have women play the part of victims, living in the sacred m-m-margins where you can worship them … (she's getting excited now) … a-a-and it makes you feel good, and reinforces your smugness about how right you are, how much b-b-better your vision is than anyone else's! But that's not really what I wanted to say. Listen, I want to say one more thing, just one thing: you say I have no political programme, well, that's just the point. I have no programme. None. I want, I want to find the unknown. Right? But if I knew how to get there I would know what it was. And if I knew what it was, it wouldn't be the unknown. So if I had a programme, as you call it, I'd never get there, I'd, I'd fail, definitely. I'd be stuck. I mean, I don't find it easy. I wish I had a, what do you call it, a programme, one that worked. Believe me, it terrifies me sometimes, waiting for the next moment, when anything could happen, it could be the unknown, at last. That's what I'm talking about. That's what you don't understand, and I'm sorry, I really am, I wish you did, but you don't.

(It's a big speech for Eye, and she falls back breathless on her saddle. Dead silence.)

John (meekly): I hear what you're saying.… And I don't have an answer. I once did, I know. But the answers are all exhausted now.

John 2: And I thought she wanted to change the world. All she's for is some vague kind of mystical trip.…

(Eye gets off the bike and goes up to John 2.)

Eye: You don't understand what I'm saying either, and you never will in a million years! You can't get it into that head of yours because it's all full of promises of money!

(John 2 grins, his eyes widen. He clutches at his head, from which disgusting eruptions are starting to appear and grow, jagged like plotted lines on a graph. Chaos, darkness. A spotlight picks out Dee, transformed to Diana. No longer in a silver

127

suit, she is sturdy and magnificent in a rosy dress, one breast exposed, wielding a symbolic bow. A loud barking and howling. Three massive hounds materialise around her, foam dripping from their lips, being restrained from making for John 2, whose face is distorting, graph-lines turned to antlers erupting and branching from his head. The darkness of the auditorium is transformed to the darkness of a forest, with perhaps a glint of water somewhere. John 2's head is now that of a stag, though he still wears his white shirt and tie and pressed trousers. He tries to escape, but the three hounds are unleashed and pursue him. At Dee/Diana's side is a smaller black dog, which Eye recognises as the one she had left to guard the entrance to the auditorium. Dee/Diana freezes the scene with a gesture.)

Dee/Diana: The world began with love. And love begins with women, the nurturers. But men have stolen love. They have fashioned it in their likeness. Because love is power. They have stolen power. They have turned love inside out. Power is no longer inside love, now love is inside power. That is what men have done. Now they rule the world. From the Arctic to the Antipodes, from industrial cities to rural communities, men subjugate women. They saw that we had power, they took it from us, in the guise of love. They use it to construct engineering works, bridges that span gulfs. Dams that destroy forests to make more power. They use it to make imaginary edifices of money, and the promise of money. They use it to build rockets, and weapons. Disgusting weapons in the shape of the phallus that are capable of disintegrating a distant city. And satellites. Satellites that survey everything and leave nothing unseen, nothing with hidden possibilities. They took it from us as love, and this is the world they made, out of money and power. Nowhere in the world can you go without this being evident. In every place of government and commerce and worship and learning. In every bedroom. But love can't really be stolen. Men think they have taken love and turned it inside out into power. But women still have love. You see these dogs? You see these dogs of mine? They are your own dogs of power, which I've turned into dogs of love that I've unleashed. Dogs? Bitches!

They scent power, because they have it in themselves. They are strong in themselves. But I've kept them apart. They have been contaminated by men's distortion of power. But now they are going to destroy it. They are going to destroy power with their love!

(John 2's head, his real head, fills the space of the arena.)

Zoo (unseen, sotto voce): I knew it. She always goes over ze top.

John 2's head: These are tedious over-simplifications and melodramatic rituals.

(The head vanishes. The dogs have caught up with the stag-headed man, and begin to maul him.)

Eye's voice: Dee, stop it. What's going on, what are you doing?

Dee/Diana (ignoring this, now become monstrous, towering over the bloody scene): I'm talking about a revolution. By those you have condemned as weak because you secretly fear the power you still haven't been able to get from them. Or because you secretly fear the weakness in yourself. Huh. Let's get down to specifics, eh? A little more than a week ago now, in the time before the future began. You brought Eye back from that party, didn't you? The Good Samaritan, or something? Bullshit! I told her she shouldn't have gone in the first place. But she said, oh, it's John, I used to know him, I told you about John. How will you get back? I said. Oh, she said, I'll go early and come back early, on the train, it's OK. I haven't seen him for five years. Midnight, and she still isn't back. One o'clock. Then the front door goes, there's this man there, all suave, he's got Eye unconscious in the car. A man? Or a dark angel? All charming manners, this angel, but I didn't trust him an inch. Oh, she passed out at the party, had too much to drink, he says. There she is in the back of the car, how did she get her clothes all wet and muddy, rumpled and torn like that, oh, he says, we found her in the garden. Who's this we? He doesn't say. And Zoo and I help her in, staggering, moaning, and he's cool as anything, what's this house, are you squatting here, none of your business, sorry I spoke. There are some odd red marks on her neck, but I don't say anything. By now I've got your number, angel, you are not what you appear, I've got your stench of power in my nostrils, under the after-shave! I'll check that she's OK next week, he says, have you got a phone here, no, I lie. I know who you are, angel. You're no Good Samaritan, you're someone who routinely uses other people as toilets. To stay with the specific, we are being specific here, uses women as toilets. Isn't that right? I know, I've met the type before, it freezes my marrow. We're not talking about your averagely routine sexist male here, we're talking danger, peril. And I put Eye to bed with my own hands, and next morning, what happened, I don't know, she says, poor girl, I had too much to drink, something happened in the garden, something happened, I wish I hadn't gone. I was watching her during the next few days. She was troubled. I felt fear for her....

(Screams. Dogs and stag-headed man have disappeared. The darkness of the forest becomes thicker.)

Eye (anxiously): Dee? What's happening?

(She's feeling dizzy, can't think straight, the boundaries to her thoughts are ill-defined, which is not an unpleasant sensation. She realises she's drunk. The darkness lifts slightly, and now she sees that the forest is not really a forest at all but an overgrown garden. Light spills from a doorway onto it. Within the house there is movement, laughter and music. She needs the coolness of the air, however, and steps out into it.

It's an early evening. The birds have not yet ceased their chatter completely. She really has had too much to drink. A spider's web lightly brushes her cheek, a bramble snags her leg. She is wearing a short black skirt and a white top, bluish in the light. Tangled paths through undergrowth, a space cleared. The smell of recent rain on the undergrowth. She needs to be alone for a minute, but there's a figure there, a tall, unfamiliar man in a fashionable suit. Darkness is on his face, then he moves into the light. He smiles and nods at her.

I saw you in there, he says. You looked as if you were all by yourself in the midst of a crowd. Oh, she says uncertainly, well, I don't know anybody here, I don't know why I came, I shouldn't have done. I don't know anybody, except John of course.

Ah, he nods, John. Of course.

Do you, do you know John, she asks timidly, are you a friend of his?

But he shakes his head. I don't know anybody either. Friend of a friend of a friend. Owners of the house.

They are now walking together down the path, he with hands thrust deep in his trouser pockets, towards the half demolished shed, hidden by bushes.

She chatters out of nervousness and drunkenness: John calls this the summer-house, apparently. He wants to rebuild it. Needs a lot of work, this garden, doesn't it? Look, where it's been cleared, those saplings. Sycamores. They come up everywhere. But he doesn't reply, he isn't interested. Sounds of the party very faint now. Well, it's the last of the summer. So let's look inside the summer-house, then, shall we? he suggests.

It's dim, and damp. Out the back, the remains of a wooden rail surrounding a verandah area. One last blackbird hops away as dusk returns. Smell of decay.

Sorry, she says, I didn't catch your name. He smiles again. John, he says, I'm John, too. She giggles, how confusing.

So have you known John, the other John, long? he presently asks.

Oh, she says. It's a long story. Well. I've known him since I was at school. We were childhood sweethearts, if you like.

How romantic, he suggests.

Not really, she replies, I mean that we weren't really childhood sweethearts, he's a good bit older than me. It didn't last long. After he went to university we stopped seeing each other. I went to a teacher training college. Then I dropped out, I couldn't take it. I bummed around, I travelled, I took jobs temping. Sometimes we wrote long letters to each other. Once he begged me to come back to him, he said he was desperate, but by then I knew it was a pose. I knew him too well, you see. Then the next thing I knew he was married. American student, she's now a journalist. She was pregnant when they married. I saw the baby — here, she falters, and he sits on the rail, which creaks alarmingly, to gaze at her. She continues: It was a very nice baby. But that was, oh, five years ago. Now I don't know, I've heard it said things are a bit rocky. She's not here, you know. The wife. I thought she would be at the party. I don't know why I came. I haven't seen him since then.

Is that why, he asks, is that why you came out into the garden? You couldn't cope with it?

Oh, she smiles dismissively, no, I just needed some air. And space. Sometimes space frightens me, sometimes I need it. My mood changes all the time. But that, that was a long time ago.

We all need air, he says, sometimes the world closes in. And now he comes closer, and places a hand lightly on her cheek. He continues: When I was a child, I'd be lying in bed ... alone ... it's all dark ... and I'd think, what if I just stopped breathing, just like that?

And immediately she feels she is choking, sobbing for breath. Surprised, he cups her face with his hands: Why are you like this? What's the matter?

He kisses her lips gently. He is her only protector. His sweet breath on her, she can even smell the toothpaste and his after-shave, just a hint. Why has she no breath of her own, because he suggested it to her, or because his breath has cancelled hers? John, don't, she says, confused, but he is kissing all over her face. Perhaps it excites him that she can't breathe, that she's sobbing for breath. Nobody can see. The party is a million miles away. Smell of decay. Pressing himself on her, she can't even breathe.

Relax, relax, he is saying, but his voice is curiously thick, conflict of message and medium, it's a different voice, not a soothing voice, as though it came from a different throat, or by a different route through his throat. He has his fingers on the soft tissue of her neck, cupping her breath, the pulse of it. How easy it would be to tighten. To put this poor suffering girl out of her misery. The thought gives him the strength he wanted. OK, so it's an illusion, who cares. Now his gentleness, what she had thought of as his gentleness, has vanished entirely, he is brutalised in an unfamiliar way, all she can think of is his name, John John, John too, he's pulling at her clothes too roughly, his two strong hands, John doubled, the darkness doubled. She's at the bottom of a well, looking up, his face fills the opening, so far away now, darkness closing over her head. Out of the darkness a vast image begins to crystallise: a six-headed apparition. The lower three heads are the heads of Diana's hounds, one glaring full-face, the other two flanking it in profile, looking to left and right. They turn into a lion's head, flanked by a wolf and a dog. Above them, the heads of John and John 2 are gazing left and right, or into the past and the future, and between them is a composite head combined from their features. As Eye looks, these heads, too, change: she recognises, with a start, her own face in the middle, flanked by that of Dee looking left and Zoo looking right. She thinks, Zoo's behind this, she's a witch, this apparition's been conjured up by Zoo. The heads change places rapidly, giving the apparition the illusion of revolving, present, past and future replacing each other. Then, suddenly, she is no longer looking on, but part of it. The auditorium appears to whirl round. For the first time, she is able dimly to see the audience, which is making whoops and catcalls. They are not people at all. The audience is composed of animals, hundreds of them sitting in rows in steeply banked concentric circles: horses, dogs, foxes, rodents, cats, even some antlered deer, birds of all kinds.)

Eye: Oh! (Closes her eyes.)

(The spinning becomes faster and faster. Can't breathe, are those fingers round her neck? Then Eye feels gentler fingers on her face.)

Zoo's voice: Wake up!

(She opens her eyes. Zoo has untied the blue silk scarf that was knotted around Eye's neck, constricting her. She smiles, and retreats. It billows out, becoming huge, enveloping her. She is on a beach, in bright sunshine, below an azure sky. In the middle of the air before her leaps a vigorous young naked Bacchus, grinning and waving a pink rag round himself. She has to smile: with a start, she recognises the boy from the petrol station, with the pony-tail. He is accompanied by Bacchantes: one, she sees, is John (whimsically resigned, with hairy animal thighs, waving an animal haunch) and the other the bearded busking violinist from the river-bank outside the concert hall (with snakes entwining his limbs, his eyebrows signalling fast and wickedly). Zoo plays the part of an attendant woman clashing a pair of cymbals, and beside her is young Nancy as a child-satyr — the small black dog accompanying them. Two cheetahs pull a small trailer, from which the Bacchus/boy has leapt. He is pointing to the sky now, above the aquamarine sea and the distant mountains. Eye looks. She sees a crown of stars.)

Nancy/satyr (whining): That's not fair. I wanted to drive the cheetahs.

Bacchus/boy: I am you and you are Eye. How's that for a neat summary? Eyeght satellites in formation for you, Eyeriadne. Coo. You lucky thing. But it ain't luck, you know. You deserve it. One day, if you like, you could come with me. Join my journey. I fancy going North this time, howz about that, dear Eye? Woodlands full of the cries of birds and the howling of wolves, light shimmering through the nearest branches. A camp fire near running water. It's always a good place to be. Then a rowing boat over dark icy cold water to them distant mountains, which're all smoky blue in the evening. Just fancy that! What d'you say?

(Eye smiles, and shakes her head regretfully.)

Bacchus/boy: No? Ah, well. It's always a possibility. For the future.

Eye: I am dreaming, aren't I?

Zoo (relaxing the cymbal-clashing pose she has struck): Naturally. We are surely all dreaming. That is the crown of your dreams.

(Mis-en-scène, or conjuring rather, by Zoo, of course. Zoo is responsible for all this. Eye now sees that crown of stars resolve itself into a spotlight. As it brightens, the brilliant scene fades to reveal the stage and the auditorium once again, its animal denizens loudly applauding.)

Eye (smiling, embarrassed): Thank you.

(But the auditorium, too, is fading, into reality beyond reality. The audience, in its steep ranks, is losing definition, becoming grey. The applause dies down. Each animal member of the audience is becoming a blank slate. An expressionless, literal blank slate. The banks of seats turn into slated roofs surrounding her. She is in a valley between two pitched roofs, under an evening sky. The spotlight becomes the moon in that sky. Before, she couldn't breathe, she was choking, sobbing for breath. But now her breath is becoming surer, more rhythmical, flooding energy back through her. And John 2 watches her from the parapet, also breathing heavily, as though he's been through some terrible ordeal. His white shirt is rumpled.)

John 2 (thick voice, as though coming from somewhere deep within him): It's what you wanted, isn't it? Isn't it? (He really wants to believe this, there's a note of desperation in his voice.) There, in the garden, behind the summer-house. You practically threw yourself upon me. Suddenly, you're sobbing, I don't know why, a pulse at your throat, I wanted to steady it, stop it, stop it forever. I wanted to still your body. You awoke something in me, something remorseless, I'll never forgive you that. Then there was something like a mist, or insubstantial water that passed between us, I wanted to force my way through it, to get to you, it was my last chance, to get to the something real that was in there, in you, somewhere, the authenticity of the earth that we stood on, if I pulled you to the earth, if I earthed you, that would help, but it didn't, you were inconceivably elusive. I had to see you again, I had to.

(They are in the car. John Newman is driving. He turns to smile at her. But she's cold, there's still a gulf between them. It's a bright autumnal day. They are driving through peaceful countryside, a stream winding below at the side of the road, willows on the banks. The road sweeps round to the left, approaching a bridge. He stops the car. "I want to take a picture here." She's his wife. Sonia is her name. They both get out. He is crashing down the bank now, brambles jagging his jacket, his expensive shoe sinking in unexpected mud, close to the river bank, to get an angle up to the bridge. She stands on the bridge above him, near the car, her small hands resting on the stone. One last smile for the camera. The picture is creased, the colours fading to blue, it falls in an irregular descent like a leaf, a long way, and enters the water below, where it's carried by the current, but nobody sees it. The sky darkens. They are on the roof, the moon above.)

John 2 (breathing heavily): Last chance ... wanted to see you again ... could think of nothing else ... couldn't stand ... your contempt ...

(But his words are drowned by a rumbling sound. Something swells in her. Is it hate, or is it blind love? Whichever it is, there is no fear. She's been purged of fear, probably. Actually, she's floating, she's a heat-seeking missile, or something equally male and terrible, reflecting back his energy upon him. She goes for him. "You don't even exist." He is regressing, visibly. No more the suit and the computers, the confident delivery. Who is he now? Her terrifying love turns him into a frightened little boy. John, John, punch the moon dead. Hit the switch. It's too dark, alone in his bed at night. Asthmatic weak boy that everybody at school jeered at, even the girls, wheezing for breath. I'll show them. I'll punish them. Who knows? His mouth open. He wets himself in his trousers, doesn't he. Ah. Poor little boy John. Baby John, all gone. You don't even exist. She begins to

•

fall forward headlong to the concrete, pushed out her hands to take the impact, crack. Breath got knocked out of her. It remained for a little while outside her body, which soon panted for it back.

Fortunately, she'd rolled. All she was aware of was something bright, spinning very fast, but slowing down.

And it was coming into focus now, as it lost its momentum gradually. A bright spinning thing. What was it? The rear wheel of her bicycle, horizontal on the ground before her. Catching the sunlight as it spun. How had it got there?

The rumbling sound almost overhead was the small shunting diesel completing its crossing of the bridge.

Eye sat up. The side of her head hurt. She put her hand to it. There was a little smear of blood, not even a trickle, though. She tested her limbs. Her right arm was scratched, bruised and bloodied, but did not seem broken or badly damaged in any other way. She leaned against the concrete and closed her eyes, taking deep breaths. A jumble of images had processed themselves through her head; it was as though she'd awoken from a dream into reality, which was the present moment, ever present and ever elusive, ever precious therefore. The hardness of the concrete beneath her, the brightness of the sky, the multiple sounds of the everyday. As if nothing had happened; but something had. It was over, though. She was tired. But she was a still centre in a whirl, a storm of confusion.

Her right leg, too, hurt. When she rolled up the trouser leg, she saw a graze all the way up her calf to her knee. She flexed it as she sat on the ground. Then, tentatively, she stood up. OK, not too bad.

She grimaced, and spoke to herself.

Eye: Serves me right, I suppose.

The diesel, retreating: Rumble, clank.

Next she inspected the bicycle. Fortunately, the wheels did not seem to have buckled, but spun freely on their axles. Too freely. That was the problem. The chain had snapped; it had sheared cleanly and now flapped uselessly, dispensing grease to her hands and ankles, the metal having been goaded beyond its last agony of fatigue by that one push on the pedal as she stormed up the slope.

If Eye had accepted the fall with philosophical stoicism as retribution for her failure of attention, she now felt the penalty had become excessive.

But there was nothing she could do. Righting the bike, therefore, she began to push it up the remainder of that slope, towards where the footpath again joined the road.

And that was not the end of it. Here, the road itself chose to resume its upward course. Wearily, Eye pushed the bike along the pavement, from time to time buffeted by the air displaced by a passing car or van. There was no other breeze here. The barren landscape shimmered.

After an hour, the road began to curve into a grove of tall trees, which afforded some respite from the autumnal sun. But if this was a relief, it was tempered by an increase in the hill's gradient. At least, it seemed that way to Eye. The perspiration was beginning to trickle down her neck, so she re-tied the silk scarf, which had come loose, around her neck. She wished she had not finished off the orange juice so early in the day.

Every now and then she imagined that the top of the hill was imminent, but each time the slight dip ahead led only to a further climb. Just when it seemed the hill could get no steeper, she at last perceived what surely must be the summit. Half-bare trees, blown into strange attitudes by a wind that was temporarily absent, stood out against the line of the ridge.

She was over the brow. As she paused, the first welcome touch of breeze caressed her hurt face.

Below, the road continued into the distance, where it met the beginnings of a large town. Suburban housing merged into more densely packed buildings, and finally some high rise blocks, all nestling/glittering between cliffs. And beyond, clouds building up in the hitherto flawless sky, and below that, haze, and a faint greyish blur on the horizon.

The sea.

Eye blinked.

She mounted the bike, and pushed off from the ground. Her feet motionless on the pedals, she began freewheeling down the hill, slowly at first, then faster as her momentum picked up, using the brakes to control the free fall. The breeze whipped her scarf.

Thus did Eye enter the coastal town that was the end of her journey, freewheeling much of the way; but occasionally having to dismount and push when the momentum gave out. In fact, it took her the rest of the afternoon to get there, the apparent nearness of the town being an optical illusion and the road concealing numerous twists and turns ahead in its approach.

But at last she was among its buildings. She glided down a wide avenue which bustled with traffic even on this early Sunday evening. She detoured the town centre, avoiding the shops, gliding slowly in the shade of an overhanging cliff dotted with holiday chalets. Clouds gathered, the sea breeze freshened. And there was the sea itself, below the coastal road, a dull, gunmetal blue flecked with white, supervised by flocks of screaming sea-gulls. Wet spots stung her face. Spray? No, not at this distance. Rain.

•

Despite the Indian summer, an inflexible law had decreed that the seaside resort should begin shutting up shop for the off-season. Already, the narrow-gauge railway along the seafront, on which throughout the summer miniature electric locomotives pulled trucks full of shrieking children, had closed down; the sheds where the locomotive and trucks lived were bolted, and the ruler-straight quarter-mile of track barely glinted under the rising clouds. However, some rides were still operating in the seafront funfair: shouts of laughter echoed from the dodgems, the aerial train still looped the loop, a variety of young children's rides still plied their trade. Coloured lights were beginning to illuminate the scene against the encroaching grey of the evening. But the big wheel stood silent, and canvas shrouded a number of the other attractions.

Pebbles and shingle, humped on the beach, hissed with every wave of the incoming tide. Nobody was swimming. A small knot of young people in shorts threw stones on the dark water, trying to make them skip in the swell. Along the promenade that bordered the beach, small boys and teenagers rode luridly painted skateboards, noisily avoiding the rows of parked cars. Traffic was still brisk, though dying, and bow-fronted hotels on the other side of the road advertised vacancies, perhaps for the first time since the spring, while fast-food restaurants remained open for business.

Eye made her way wearily along the seafront, wheeling her

bike. The brief squall of rain had stopped, but it was colder now and the wind came in from the sea. She had put on another layer of clothing, but not yet her coat. Ahead of her the pier was illuminated. Evening business was commencing on one of the last Sundays of the season. There was a helter-skelter at the other end of the pier, all lit up like a lighthouse, and among the tacky stalls a pretentious palm court restaurant, half-full. A man bawled from the shooting range, and a disc jockey blared embarrassing messages from the bingo hall, between the Top Forty hits.

A plastic Wishing Well invited holidaymakers to contribute their pennies to the fund for a well-known children's hospital; as Eye watched, a small child tearfully begged its mother to allow it to toss in a coin. No, the mother was saying, we have to go home now. And anyway, that hospital already has enough money. The child insisted. Oh all right, just one.

When they had gone, Eye wandered over to the Wishing Well. She looked over. There was real water at the bottom, where hundreds of coins glinted.

She rummaged in the shoulder bag that was strapped to the bike, and removed the remainder of the bundle of banknotes. Making sure no-one was looking, she dropped the bundle into the well. The paper money began to uncurl under water. Soon it would be a soggy mess. But perhaps usable when dried out.

She bumpily wheeled the bike over the wooden slats of the pier. You could see the waves boiling below, between the slats. It reminded her of that footbridge in the city, from which she had thrown the alien wallet into the river.

Another small child, under the supervision of its parents, was gleefully tossing the remnants of a sandwich off the side of the pier onto the waters. As each piece of bread was launched, gulls swooped in, apparently from nowhere, shrieking hysterically. Eye leaned over the side and watched the gulls on the water for some time. Dead sailors.

Then she guided the bike down a ramp towards the beach. The smell of hot dogs and hamburgers assailed her. Suddenly, realising she had had nothing to eat all day, she became hungry.

At beach level, she bought a hamburger at a stall beside a noisy amusement arcade. Wanting to avoid the electronic howls of the machines — horses, spaceships, racing cars, games of chance — she took it out to the shingle. She rested the bike against a low wall under the pier and sat beside it, munching the burger and gazing out to sea. The sun had gone down now, but in any case it would have been invisible behind the vast clouds that swelled from the horizon.

A small black dog was snuffling about the wet shingle where the waves broke. Although it had a collar on, there was no sign of its owners. It was an eager mongrel, unnoticed by the throng as it investigated the shore line.

Eye picked out a piece of driftwood and threw it over the dog's head into the sea. It arched, and plopped. Instantly, the dog began to wag its tail. It plunged recklessly into the breaking waves, adding its little something to the splashes. Then it paddled, nose outstretched, to where the stick bobbed, clamped its teeth firmly on it, swerved round and sped on the short journey back to the shore, where it gave itself a vigorous shake, still clutching the stick, before trotting complacently up to where Eye sat and dropping it before her. It waited with some eagerness, its brown eyes gazing, limbs flexed for action. Eye got to her feet, picked up the wood and threw it further this time. The dog raced away in a loud hiss of shingle, plunged back into the water, and retrieved it a second time. Its tail was a wet blur as it anticipated Eye's third throw.

With all her strength, she flung it high into the air. It sailed over the waves, but this time it was off course, and hit one of the pier supports with a small crack before dropping into the oily scum. The dog paddled away. It paddled around the pier support, hunting for the bobbing stick.

Eye's attention was distracted by a tanker crossing her line of vision on the horizon, blurred by mist. After a few moments, when she looked for the dog again, she realised something was wrong. She could see the dog paddling furiously in the shadow of the pier. But it seemed not to be moving. The more it paddled, the more it seemed to stay in the same place.

When she got down to the edge of the water, she saw the problem. Somehow, the dog had become entangled in a fragment of oily netting attached to the pier strut. It was trying vainly to get away. Every so often a wave of the incoming tide washed over its head. It was uttering astonishingly discreet yelps. Appalled, Eye took off her shoes and socks and rolled her trousers up, hardly noticing the rosy graze from her fall that adorned her right leg. She waded out into the water, which stung and chilled. She had to be careful, because it was slippery underfoot.

At last, she reached the poor dog. The waves lapped over her trousers, reaching her thighs; occasionally a bigger one sprayed her. The water was unpleasantly greasy. Her chilled fingers tried to work the dog free from the strands of netting. It squirmed and splashed, making the task more difficult. She thought of the power in her hands. How easy it would be to tighten her grip, to steady the dog's struggles, hold it down as wave after wave came over it. To watch its brown eyes plead in misery, to put it gently out of the very misery she'd created. Its eyes watching her from a great distance, from a place of no air, the water between her and it, and she watching it slipping away into darkness. She shuddered. The tangle of netting was hard. But finally she had it figured out. Immediately, the dog made for the shore, and she followed clumsily splashing.

The dog jumped up happily at her as she put her shoes and socks back on. It wanted to continue the game.

"That's it — no more," said Eye firmly, as though talking to a child. She was cold and wet now as well as tired and hurt. Time to move on. She retrieved the useless bicycle and started to push it off the beach and up the ramp towards the promenade again. The dog followed at her heels, sometimes pausing to give itself another shake, to try and get the sea out of its fur.

Eye stopped to pat it. She looked round. There was still no sign of an owner. She murmured to it: "You can't come with me, old thing. Why, I don't even like dogs that much, to tell the truth."

The dog: !?!

There was no shaking it off. She turned, and continued to push the bike up to the promenade. She crossed the road at the traffic lights. And the dog faithfully trotted behind her.

•

What did Eye learn, if anything, from the short episode of saving the dog from drowning? The power of a gratuitous act, above all. An act of love or violence is one that changes the world, probably irrevocably, for good or ill (if you need to think about in those terms) — because such an act leaves unpredictable resonances in the world's physics and chemistry that could have disproportionate consequences, you can't tell. There is a residue, in other words. Sometimes the residue remains unperceived for a very long time.

Was the dog grateful? No, of course not. Gratitude is a human concept, tainted through with hypocrisy. Love, perhaps. Not even that. You can't say love. The act of saving the dog established a focus for the binding relationships that keep the world together, that keep it from falling asunder. Eye sometimes thought the word "magic". She didn't really know what that was, other than some kind of relationship. A way of relating, nothing more. Something gets ravelled, something else gets unravelled. But the bonds are not imprisoning bonds, they're skeins of light, not even light, something much faster than, much lighter than light. You can't see them if you look for them.

Did the episode change her ideas about time? Not substantially. Her ideas about time had been evolving long before that, and whenever she tried to express them they just came out as clumsy metaphors anyway, as they were bound to do. And then everybody misunderstood, including herself at times. That is, she misled herself, and everything became that much more difficult. But action does eclipse thought, and substitutes an unanticipated moment for an expected one; the "present" and the "future" change places, the whole of it happening in such a dizzying flash as to bypass understanding. If anything, she would be less inclined from now on to try and express her ideas as metaphors, recognising the folly of this strategy, but whether saving the dog had anything to do with it even she couldn't answer.

Had it changed her body language? Her body language had already been changed by: time; displacement in space; knowledge; weariness; physical constraints. The vigour had leaked out of her step for now; she pushed the bicycle up the hill and away from the sea with little enthusiasm, little physical sense that she had reached the end of her journey. The dog, by contrast, was chipper enough; it plunged its nose towards every drain it passed, cocked its leg at every lamp-post; trotted off at every possible tangent that offered a new scent; and always came back to Eye and her bicycle as its reference point, its ground bass.

The hill was lined on both sides with brick terraced houses, steeply serried as though they were two fanned packs of cards waiting for their trick.

As Eye climbed, she saw a middle-aged woman in a pink coat, a headscarf and walking boots coming down the pavement towards her from the top of the hill. It was a familiar figure.

The middle-aged woman, in her turn, saw a weary young woman, slim, with short dark hair, pushing a muddied three-speed bicycle up the hill.

When she got nearer she saw the young woman had a graze on the side of her face and bruises on her right forearm, visible where the sweatshirt sleeve had. been pushed up. Her trousers were wet, and moisture had travelled to her shoes, removing patches of their accumulated dust. The blue scarf round her neck was stained with perspiration. To her, the young woman was also shockingly familiar.

She stopped short first, and then, hesitatingly, quickened her pace till the two met.

"Eileen," was all she said. Then they embraced wordlessly. Then: "Look at you. What on earth have you been up to?" But Eye just smiled ruefully.

"Well come in and have a cup of tea, and get those wet things off," ordered the woman.

They proceeded a little way further up the hill — the middle-aged woman retracing part of her steps — then soundlessly turned in at one of the houses, and mounted the few steps together, Eye hauling the bike, the woman fumbling for the front door key in her bag. But Eye remembered something.

Eye: Oh, I seem to have accidentally picked up this dog which has lost its owner. Do you mind if it comes in with me?

The woman: What dog?

Eye looked. No dog. She descended the steps again, and looked up and down the street. No sign of it.

Eye: You didn't see a black dog following me?

The woman: No, dear.

Eye (shrugging): Oh, well.

They went through the hall with its blushing pink carpet, where Eye left the bike and the woman her coat, and into the kitchen, where she slumped on a chair. Old-fashioned, portable radio on the fridge. Everything familiar. As it always was.

The woman: Well, you were in luck. A little earlier and I would have been out on the downs, taking my Sunday afternoon walk. You know, I've kept it up every single Sunday afternoon, since your father died. It's … well, I suppose it's just a habit, nothing more.

Eye received this is silence.

The woman (brightening): Now, shall I put the kettle on?

Eye: Please.

The woman: You're really wiped out, aren't you? You should have told me you were coming, you silly girl. Never mind. We'll have a nice cup of tea, then you can tell me to what I owe the honour. (Suddenly apprehensive lest this should be taken amiss:) But I'm really so pleased to see you.

Eye: It's nice to come home.

The woman: Living such a hand to mouth existence as you do. Always one thing after another. But there, I won't nag. You'll run away again if I do. I know I'm always nagging you, I'm always telling you you should think about your future.

•

I don't know what Eileen meant when she told her mother she would like to stay for "a while"; how far she had anticipated events, what final analysis she had arrived at about her predicament. Did she know then, or had she guessed, that already the germ of a new life had begun to grow, or glow, out of zero — out of the zero within her? At all events, she didn't tell her mother until some time later, when it became irrefutable; and her mother accepted it with surprising equanimity, perhaps even glad above all that she would now be needed by her daughter, that she would have a role to play once more.

It's possible Eileen did know. There are things you know, deep within your body, and that knowledge comes from the same mysterious zero to which it finally returns.

Her mother had preserved Eileen's childhood bedroom intact, almost as though it were a museum piece. No, not a museum piece, because that implies something frozen in time, a window on the past, its use value cancelled; whereas Eileen's bedroom had the permanent air of awaiting. That is, awaiting her return. There isn't an inevitability about this. Things might have turned out differently than they did. It was a possibility that had been left open, and one that, in the event, had been fulfilled.

What was the bedroom like? Not too dissimilar to the one she had left in the city. About the same size, a small, square room with a low ceiling, but more conventional in proportions, lacking the attic-style window, and facing (across the back gardens) a row of houses exactly similar to the one this was part of. You can imagine: battered and half-forgotten soft toys lining a shelf, the faint outlines on the yellow-wallpapered walls where posters had once been blue-tacked, a jumble of adolescent clothes in the wardrobe drawer, a Mickey Mouse alarm clock beside the narrow bed with its candlewick bedspread. Everything seemed to her so much smaller than she remembered.

Eileen also retrieved a small table from the loft, which she set up by the window. I imagine that she sat there quite a lot, gazing out into the garden and writing in her Chinese notebook.

That first evening, she went to bed at ten o'clock, and slept for twelve hours. But not before her mother had insisted on her having at least sandwiches and a mug of beefy drink on a tray in front of the television. The brief Sunday evening news bulletin contained a report that interested her: "Pieces of a landmapping satellite fell into the Pacific Ocean this morning, say scientists who have been tracking its course since it began to deviate from its orbit last Thursday...."

In the next few days there were things to sort out. Mending her bike was one. On Monday morning she phoned the office in the city to say she was not coming in again. Then she took the precaution of signing on at the local unemployment office before looking for a typing job locally which would tide her over for a while. That expression again: "a while". Useful in its lack of specificity.

With some apprehension, she also phoned the house. She didn't know quite what it was she dreaded to hear. The phone rang for a good minute before Dee picked it up. She sounded surprised and worried. Are you all right? Yes, Eileen assured her, what about you? Yes, said Dee. Is everything OK in the house? said Eileen. Fine, no problem. Are you sure? Eileen wanted to know. If anything, you know, funny turns up, let me know at once (she didn't really know how to frame the request — there were just still some possibilities left unaccounted for — which made it confusing for Dee). Hey, said Dee, changing the subject, we had this letter this morning which was an amazing amount of money, was that anything to do with you, Eye? Yes, said Eileen, keep it, but can you do me a favour?

She asked Dee if she could get her "things" sent on. It would only require the hire of a small van. Dee was astonished, speechless even for a rare moment in her life.

Eileen: Just the clothes and books and cassettes mainly. Not any of the furniture, and you can keep the kitchen things.

Dee: OK. Well, I'm sorry about that. About your not coming back, I mean. Are you sure you're all right?

Eileen: Yes, fine. I will be back some time. I'll see you some time. Give my love to Zoo.

Time went by. The hardest decision Eileen had to make was not to contact John at the farmhouse. Were he to hear of her pregnancy, he would be hard to resist. And that would be bad news. She still didn't feel strong enough in herself to resist his quiet reason.

Coming home — and she was surprised to find she still thought of it as that — was something she judged at times as an admission of failure, in some sense, and at other times as a tactical retreat, a gathering of strength until she could face the outside world again. Which she knew she would have to, sooner or later. That world that was slowly being reassembled in her mind, the world of the past that gave substance to the present. In the meantime — this precious present time — there were quiet pleasures to be enjoyed.

I expect she did a little gardening, getting the small back garden into shape, which had been difficult for her mother with the back trouble she'd recently been experiencing. She enjoyed that.

Her mother was commendably restrained in her enquiries. She didn't press for details of the father after Eileen had told her she had "never seen him again", nor did she even express any moral disapproval, sensing perhaps the presence of something bigger than could reasonably be articulated, something they would both have difficulty in coming to terms with, making of discretion the better part of wisdom. Once, when she asked Eileen why she had left the city, and the house in which she had been squatting ("such an awful word, squatting"), Eileen replied simply: "The house had a ghost in it."

Every evening they watched TV together. Once, while she was in the kitchen, Eileen thought she heard the news bulletin she'd been dreading. It would have been on the regional news, and, though Eileen would still have found difficulty precisely formulating its possibilities, it would have gone something like this: "Police are still looking for/have been making house to house searches/have found the body of missing commodities broker John Newman, whose car was found abandoned such and such weeks ago…" She rushed into the living room, heart beating rapidly, startling her mother, but it was nothing, some other story entirely, she must have imagined the words she'd overheard.

Towards Christmas, soon after she had confirmed and broken to her mother the news of her pregnancy, Eileen received a letter from Zoo. It was postmarked Germany.

"My dear Ei, I have not many news to tell you since I am back here in Germany," it began. "It's so boring after you left! Diana was in bad mood a great deal, you know, she got into her reckless phrases, although I think she has recovered now. She actually got a job! But then my money has run out, so I returned, I got a job in an artgallery here, it's OK. I'm going with a boy called Klaus who plays the guitar in a band. Some times I sing a little with the band, we play in clubs et cetera. How are you? Write me and tell me your news, please!

"You know, after that morning when I couldn't find the book I never get the chance to make your Tarot reading, so I had the idea to make it myself for you. I did it before I leave. And here is what I discovered.

"The first card is the Fool! Now, don't be surprised, that doesn't mean you are foolish. The Fool can mean lots of things. He is Madman or Genius, and also he represents Chaos and Outsider. But the other side is, he is immortal and transformed by spiritual knowledge. It is a very significant card, it's from what they call the Major Arcana. I think it means, Ei, that you are a very special person. You have gifts that maybe few persons have.

"But what do those gifts mean? Well, the second card is Six of Cups. That means it's possible for you to achieve harmony in the future. Strange things happen in the past, but they can influence your future for good. The new things in your life are linked to the past. You alone can tell what that means.

"However, there is a warning. The third card is the King of Swords reversed. That can mean Chaos too, so it warns again of the bad side of the Fool. It means too cruelty and the bad side of the intellect. Possibly that is a danger in yourself but more likely you are exposed to danger by some other person you trust.

"The next card shows the past cause of the present situation. It's Ten of Swords. That is a bad card. It means the lowest point in the cycle of fortune. But also it means that things can only get better. I think you have something bad happened to you recently, but the worst is over, happily.

"What about the future? The next card is Seven of Swords reversed. To go back to the Fool and Six of Cups, it's a warning that you could fail to attain spiritual knowledge and harmony. You could surrender when the victory is almost attained. That's the danger. You must still carry through a brave action.

"Please do write, my dear Ei, I'm always glad to hear from you. Maybe one day you visit me here!

"Your dear friend, Susannah."

A smile flickered on Eileen's face as she sat at her little table re-reading the letter, written in purple ink on thick recycled green paper with deckled edges. "You must still carry through a brave action." One of her regrets (though she wasn't sure how much she believed in this sort of thing any more) was that she had not got to know Zoo better in the few months they had lived together in the house.

Fear was beginning to leave her.

Outside, rain was falling steadily on the garden.

•

Eighteen months after the events of that autumn, Eileen returned to the city and to the house.

It was a lovely spring morning, the sky a pure china blue, a lazy breeze coquettishly tickling, and even here in the inner city the scent of new-mown grass from the park insinuating itself in the hurrying crowds' nostrils. Eileen had bought a day return rail ticket from the coast. The child was still young enough to travel free.

This time, she was not pushing a bicycle but a candy-striped buggy on which the child, newly promoted from its pram, wriggled and gurgled in its own individual rhythm. From time to time, Eileen smiled at it, or uttered a soft sound, low on semantic meaning but high on emotional content. Sometimes the child would take no notice; at other times, it paused, assessing the communication, then its face broke out into the elicited grin.

She turned into the lane, its three great plane trees already well advanced in new leafage. At the other end was the grim school, from which she could faintly hear the sounds of children laughing and screaming in the hidden playground. Cars were parked nose-to-tail all the way up to it. The low brick wall was exactly as she remembered it, still bearing the faded shaky words THIS IS NOT A DUMP. Right in front of this, as though to illustrate some paradox, black plastic bags were piled, some spilling their rancid content onto the broken pavement. Pieces of an old wooden bedstead and a dead television set were stacked beside.

On the right hand side was the house. Eileen paused, her heart sinking.

It was still intact, between the scrubby bit of greenery and the fenced-off car-park, with its odd pair of half-gables, the only house left of a terrace that had once occupied the entire lane. But something had happened.

Eileen wished she had kept in touch by phone more often. By the time she had got round to deciding to pay a visit, the number had yielded only the "unobtainable" signal. Still, she'd decided to come. Perhaps, she told herself, Dee had been unable to pay the phone bill and it had been cut off.

Where once there was a front door (to which she still had a key) now a sheet of galvanised corrugated iron barred the way. Iron also stopped up all the windows on the ground floor. The upper windows were dark and lifeless, including the little attic window just below the roof that had once belonged to her bedroom. Notices pasted onto the corrugated iron promised the public that the house was due to be "redeveloped" by the municipal authorities, and warned of the dire consequences of trespass.

Eileen paused far longer than was necessary to read this message. A soft gurgle from the child jerked her out of her pause.

She wheeled the push-chair round the side of the house and through the narrow alleyway formed between the wall and the chain-link fencing of the car-park. Shadow fell here at this time of day. The gate leading to the back yard had been newly padlocked. But despite the minatory notices someone had neatly sawn through the padlock. She pushed, and the gate fell open.

The small back yard was a mess. Rubble and wood had been dumped on it in great quantities. The only other sign of activity, if such it was, was that the corrugated iron on the back window had been ripped off the window-frame on one side and bent right back. She could peer right into the big through room that she, Zoo and Dee had once used as their living room. It was deserted.

She tried the sash, which stuck at first, but finally was persuaded squeakily to ease itself upward three feet. She called through: Is anyone there? Faint echo of her words, no other response.

Quickly unbuckling the child, which was distracted by a small woollen rabbit she produced out of her shoulder bag, she folded the push-chair and pushed it through the window. She gathered some stray bricks to build a platform, grasped the child under its armpits and hauled herself astride the window-ledge. Then she was able to drop the child gently inside the room, and swing over herself.

She peered through the gloom. Part of the now bare floor-boards had been ripped up, showing the joists beneath, and there were ashes in the gaping fireplace that was newly revealed by the ripping out of the gas fire. Soot stains on the surrounds suggested that the chimney had not coped well.

She picked up the child, who was beginning to whimper, and soothed it with one-way conversation. Then, steadily, apprehensively, she made her way to the hall, where once her bicycle had lived. Smell of damp and urine. The stairs were dark, but light drifted from the upper floors, where the windows had not been blocked up. She called again. No response but the echo of her voice. She began to mount.

The first-floor kitchen was a mess, with large parts of flooring missing. Only the cooker remained. The bath had been taken out of the bathroom, and the toilet smashed apparently with a sledge-hammer.

She reached the top. Her attic bedroom.

It was completely bare, but intact. Morning light poured through the smeared glass of the little, odd-shaped window.

I have said that fear began to leave Eileen shortly after she went to stay at her mother's on the coast. But it hadn't gone completely away, and as she sat in the middle of the floor of her erstwhile bedroom, playing with her child and its woollen rabbit, a silent dread entered her, filled her and returned weakness to her limbs. She gazed at the ceiling. It horrified, fascinated and attracted her. Something remained. A last action that could not be avoided.

She took a small blanket from her shoulder bag, spread it on the floor, dotted it with toys, and spoke to the child.

Eileen: Just play here, will you? Are you going to be good? Just play here while Mummy does something.

The child (cheerfully): Nyerr-err.

Amazingly, the ladder was still in its cupboard just outside the room. She fitted it into place, climbed. She felt sick, and dizzy. Keep a grip on yourself. Push. Don't think.

Stiffly, the trapdoor opened, letting light from the sky flood down. She pushed it as far as it would go. A clatter almost stopped her heart. It was pigeons, startled out of their rest, fluttering off.

She was in the valley between the pitched roofs. In the intervening eighteen months more slates had worked themselves loose; some had slid all the way down to the centre gully. Her legs were trembling so much she was in imminent danger of kicking the ladder away beneath her, so she climbed all the way through.

There was nothing to be seen.

But there was something. A rumpled and faded tartan blanket on the slates. She picked it up. It had the stiffness of repeated soaking and drying by the weather. She shook it out.

Another object, almost unrecognisable at first. A curled, yellowed thing. A paperback book about the Tarot. Zoo's book.

It was peaceful here, under the blue morning sky. Then she heard the child down below start to wail.

•

Eileen lay back on the old tartan blanket on the roof. She didn't close her eyes as she had once done, because the child was playing among the slates and had to be watched the whole time in case it did itself an injury.

Smiling, she picked it up and cuddled it. It laughed happily.

For a long time, a weight of fear had oppressed her. Now it was as though bit by bit the fear was leaving her through the top of her head, evaporating into the peaceful space of the sky. And she could contemplate it, that empty, limitless sky. Perhaps because the child anchored her to the earth.

She took the child to the parapet, from which they could see her beloved horizon: there it all was, morning sunlight shone on the office blocks, the housing estate, the communications tower and the cathedral. Above them, a drone. An airliner, tiny and flashing, was carrying its load of passengers from the other side of the world to the international airport beyond the city. "Look," she said, pointing, but the child squirmed and wanted to be put down. So she lowered it gently into the safety of the gully. It began to crawl, jerkily, towards the woollen rabbit.

She loved the child.

No, that isn't quite adequate.

I've said that fear left Eileen. I don't know if this is true. It's likely that at least some does remain; that it will always be there. For example, her intense love for the child. Is there something frightening about this? Is it generated out of intense sadness? I can't say. There is something inscrutable about her and her emotions. I imagine her feelings of love and fear rising to a peak every now and then, and leaving her heart beating that much faster. Where do those feelings come from? From the same nothingness, the same zero from which the child itself appeared and grew?

There is a great deal that can't be determined, that remains in the zone of uncertainty. If this weren't so, if the known were all there was, no movement would be possible from any single imagined moment.

And I can only imagine that moment. The smell of the child, its soft limbs, its tremendous, sought-after smile, its cry from the heart. This holds Eileen more powerfully even than the blue space of the sky above the rooftop. She watches it now, as it plays with the woollen animal, putting it experimentally in its mouth. Something is always happening: peaking, then falling away, each a unique event that nevertheless sends out ripples of consequence, for the first and last time. These events with uncertain outcome — I can no longer describe them, let alone assess their significance beyond the blank page at the end of this. This: my imagining of her surge of love for the child — and the realisation that, after all, she can feel such love.

Other titles in print from Reality Street:

Poetry series
Tony Baker: *In Transit,* £7.50
Nicole Brossard: *Typhon Dru,* £5.50
Cris Cheek/Sianed Jones: *Songs From Navigation,* £12.50
Kelvin Corcoran: *Lyric Lyric,* £5.99
Ken Edwards: *eight + six,* £7.50
Allen Fisher: *Dispossession and Cure,* £6.50
Allen Fisher: *Place,* £18
Susan Gevirtz: *Taken Place,* £6.50
Jim Goar: *Seoul Bus Poems,* £7.50
Bill Griffiths: *Collected Earlier Poems (1966-80),* £18
Jeff Hilson: *stretchers,* £7.50
Jeff Hilson (ed.): *The Reality Street Book of Sonnets,* £15
Anselm Hollo (ed. & tr.): *Five From Finland,* £7.50
Horwitz/Edwards (ed.): *Botsotso: contemporary South African poetry,* £12.50
Fanny Howe: *O'Clock,* £6.50
Fanny Howe: *Emergence,* £7.50
Peter Jaeger: *Rapid Eye Movement,* £9.50
Tony Lopez: *Data Shadow,* £6.50
David Miller: *Spiritual Letters (I-II),* £6.50
Wendy Mulford: *The Land Between,* £7.50
Redell Olsen: *Secure Portable Space,* £7.50
Maggie O'Sullivan: *In the House of the Shaman,* £6.50
Maggie O'Sullivan: *Body of Work,* £15
Maggie O'Sullivan (ed.): *Out of Everywhere,* £12.50
Sarah Riggs: *chain of minuscule decisions in the form of a feeling,* £7.50
Denise Riley: *Mop Mop Georgette,* £6.50
Denise Riley: *Selected Poems,* £9
Peter Riley: *Excavations,* £9
Lisa Robertson: *Debbie: an Epic,* £7.50*
Lisa Robertson: *The Weather,* £7.50*
Maurice Scully: *Steps,* £6.50
Maurice Scully: *Sonata,* £8.50
Robert Sheppard: *The Lores,* £7.50
Lawrence Upton: *Wire Sculptures,* £5
Carol Watts: *Wrack,* £7.50

* co-published with New Star Books, Vancouver, BC

4Packs series

1: *Sleight of Foot* (Miles Champion, Helen Kidd, Harriet Tarlo, Scott Thurston), £5

2: *Vital Movement* (Andy Brown, Jennifer Chalmers, Mike Higgins, Ira Lightman), £5

3: *New Tonal Language* (Patricia Farrell, Shelby Matthews, Simon Perril, Keston Sutherland), £5

4: *Renga+* (Guy Barker, Elizabeth James/Peter Manson, Christine Kennedy), £5

Narrative series

Ken Edwards: *Nostalgia for Unknown Cities,* £8.50

Paul Griffiths: *let me tell you,* £9

John Hall: *Apricot Pages,* £6.50

Richard Makin: *Dwelling,* £15

David Miller: *The Dorothy and Benno Stories,* £7.50

Douglas Oliver: *Whisper 'Louise',* £15

Reality Street depends for its continuing existence on the Reality Street Supporters scheme. For details of how to become a Reality Street Supporter, or to be put on the mailing list for news of forthcoming publications, write to the address on the reverse of the title page, or email **info@realitystreet.co.uk**

Visit our website at: **www.realitystreet.co.uk**